FORTUNE'S
FOOL

FORTUNE'S FOOL

Kathleen Karr

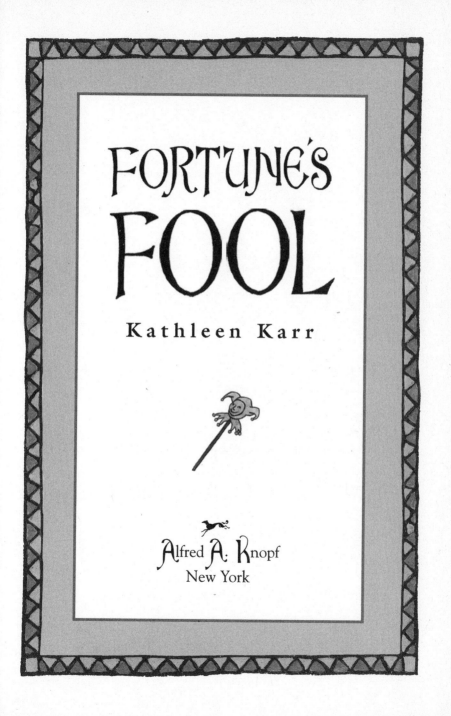

Alfred A. Knopf
New York

Published in the United States by Alfred A. Knopf, an imprint of
Random House Children's Books, a division of Random House, Inc., New York.

Knopf, Borzoi Books, and the colophon are registered trademarks
of Random House, Inc.

Visit us on the Web! www.randomhouse.com/kids

Educators and librarians, for a variety of teaching tools, visit us at
www.randomhouse.com/teachers

Library of Congress Cataloging-in-Publication Data
Karr, Kathleen.
Fortune's fool / Kathleen Karr. — 1st ed.
    p. cm.
Summary: In medieval Germany, fifteen-year-old Conrad, a court jester, and his beloved
Christa, a servant girl, escape from a cruel master and journey through the countryside on a
quest to find a kind lord who will give them sanctuary.
ISBN 978-0-375-84816-2 (trade) — ISBN 978-0-375-94816-9 (lib. bdg.)
[1. Adventure and adventurers—Fiction. 2. Fools and jesters—Fiction. 3. Dwarfs—Fiction.
4. Christian life—Fiction. 5. Germany—History—1273–1517—Fiction.] I. Title.
PZ7.K149For 2008
[Fic]—dc22
2007049034

Printed in the United States of America
May 2008

10 9 8 7 6 5 4 3 2 1

First Edition

For Christine and Antony—
good friends, well met

ONE

I follow in the handsprings of my father. He was known as Hans the Large, but in the end, I fear his girth confounded even his mirth, leaving me—

"**C**onrad!"

The flick of a whip caught my inkpot, near emptying it before it be plugged. Better another stroke to my back. Ink was dear.

"Fool! Do I feed you to scribble?"

Stuffing quill and parchment in my pouch, I leaped from the stones of the courtyard into a somersault. "As you can neither read nor write, who better than your fool, my lord?"

My idiot master's face turned purple with displeasure. It became necessary to execute an entire series of cartwheels around his gross form. Bells jangling, I defied his whip with my speed and set him into dizziness. Having achieved my revenge, I stopped and shook the belled ass's ears of my cap for good measure, then offered a grin. "Hey, *da derry, diddle, day, ay* . . . How spend you this Feast of John Chrysostom day?"

Otto of Schwarzenberg steadied himself with a growl. "In hunting, numbskull, as every fine day—and all possible between. Bestir yourself before the light be gone."

Flipping into a handstand, I made my way to the stables upside down. Blood rushing into my head always improved my thinking. Saint John Chrysostom, "the Golden-mouthed," was by way of being my patron. I must pray well to him this day, for fat Otto was growing weary of my tongue. Upright again, I readied my mount as my thoughts raced on.

To play the fool is not the role I would have chosen in life. Yet having been born to it, I must make the best of the jest laid upon me. Just so had I been doing for the fullness of my fifteen years.

My horse stamped a hoof impatiently.

"Nay, Blackspur. Keep your peace. Truth be told, I wager a mighty charger you would be, and I a shining squire leading you into battle." I tightened his bellyband and gave him a fond pat. "In Heaven, mayhap. Till then, we must entertain our dullard masters upon this Middle Earth."

So Blackspur and I rode to the hunt instead of into battle. Yet it was battle of a kind. Retainers vied among themselves for position to bring up Otto's rear. Hounds nipped one another in forming their own processional. None of this concerned me, as I always rode at my master's side. But such favor held its price. Once through the compound's gate and down the winding lane past the shabby village hugging its moated walls, I was expected to perform. As we reached the fields spread over the plateau beyond the castle's crag, I nudged Blackspur onto the already well-trampled path through what remained of the peasants' autumn harvest and spoke in his ear.

"Now, my friend."

Blackspur broke into the exaggerated motions I had schooled him in. As his forelegs rose in the high-stepping gait of a true charger, I held my marotte before me like a shield. Shaking its bladder of dried peas, I cried, "*Charge! Forward to Glory!*"

On cue, Blackspur charged mightily, as if facing all the Saracens of the Holy Land . . . halted in midstride with a jolt, then kicked up his rear legs like a mule—tossing me through a wide arc into the rye.

"Ho!" Otto bellowed.

"Ha!" his retainers joined in—though I'd performed the same feat on every hunt since the beginning of autumn.

Ignoring the new aches, I shoved aside baying hounds and leaped from my bed of grasses to make my bow for Otto. "*Hey, nonny, no*, a-hunting I must go!"

"And so you will!"

Still snickering, Otto flipped a coin at me, which I caught adroitly with another bow. Then I slipped a carrot reward to my waiting Blackspur and remounted with relief. Today's fall had gone well. I was back in Otto of Schwarzenberg's good favor. I sent up a prayer to Heaven and my patron saint.

Lord Jesus, good Saint John, grant me the grace to survive the remainder of this day.

Otto's hunting party mauled its way across the remnants of the fields to the dark line of forest waiting beyond. Every fox and hare of full wit scattered in advance.

Night's chill closed in around Otto's banqueting hall. I shivered within the garishly painted colors of my woolen tunic. It would be a cold, early winter. Otto seemingly felt none of it. His great black beard glistened from wiping his fingers upon it between wolflike bites into the haunch clutched in one fist and swinish attacks upon the beaker of ale gripped in the other. But then he was seated on the dais with his lady, Ermengud, beside him—and the roaring fireplace at his back. In the drafts among the lower tables lining the walls, I inched closer to boards holding wooden platters of rapidly disappearing sausages—till Otto belched a belch that echoed through the rafters, then set down his ale.

"*Music!*" he roared.

A sausage disappeared into my purse as out came my pipe. I bowed to Otto. "A boon of ale to wet my whistle and sweeten the music, my lord!"

Otto pointed a greasy finger at a serving girl. "Drink for the fool, wench!"

4

My boon arrived with a whisper. "Cook is keeping dinner for you, Conrad."

I smiled at my equally ill-used comrade and gave Christa's flaxen braid a playful tweak. "Keep clear of the monster's pinches tonight, little sparrow. He's been a bear the whole day."

"Would they were yours, Conrad." With a sudden blush, she hoisted her tray to the next table.

As for me, I wet my whistle and began to play. Only after I had danced through my entire repertoire thrice over, only after Otto had crammed the last of a magnificent quince pie down his gullet and licked each finger in turn—would that Cook had saved a taste for me—only then was I nearly excused for the night.

Otto eased his expanded belly away from the boards. "Well played, fool," he pronounced. "You may set to with your supper."

"Thank you, good master!" I fawned with a jingling flip of delight. Then off I crawled to the nearest pile of bones being contended over by the hounds. Their pleasure at my encroachment equaled my own.

"Save your snarl, Fang," I growled at the nearest as I wrestled a well-gnawed joint from his control. "It's all a play, and it's past time you learned your role in the farce."

To the muted threats of my master's favorites, I brought the feast to my mouth and made a show of savoring it. On his dais above, Otto clapped with glee.

I staggered with a groan to the stables and my bed of straw next to the dozing Blackspur. There'd been no quince pie in the kitchen, but the ever-bubbling cauldron of pottage, thick with cabbage and oats, had filled my stomach well enough. And the snatched sausage would breakfast me. At last, I could yank off my fool's cap . . . run fingers through my short-cropped hair . . . and begin the final task of the day.

"Blackspur," I murmured, picking lice from my cap, "the night is too short to make amends for the day. Life is too short to atone for its injustices."

To a whinny of sympathy, I laid my weary body down.

TWO

I was born of the Black Death. Born and damned both. Priests call the pestilence the good God's rod to beat His erring children. Yet how can God be good and set such affliction upon His family? How can God be good and orphan such as me before the honey of my mother's milk e'er be tasted? How could His Son, our Lord Jesus, be less forgiving than a petty earthly lordling?

Rain pounded the stable's slates above my head as I slumped in my usual Sabbath gloom. I reached for the forbidden knife buried beneath the straw and began to mend my quill point. Witless Otto and his court knelt within his chapel's walls hearing Mass, being shriven of their sins, receiving sacred sacraments. Without the castle walls, peasants and shopkeepers knelt in unison beneath the steeple of Saint Hedwig's Church. Why, then, was I denied such succor?

"Make peace with it, Conrad," my father had urged on his deathbed. "Holy Mother Church has not a sense of humor."

Make peace with it. Why should jesters—even minstrels—be thought damned for bringing a little joy into this sad world? How to make peace with my father's unmarked and unconsecrated grave? How to make peace with my unbaptized soul?

Blackspur nickered above me.

"Less said, friend. There should be better uses put to my only hours of rest."

Rolling my sheet of parchment with its brothers, I stuffed my fool's cap in my belt, turned my tunic inside out, the better to still its bells, and headed forth into the cold rain.

Save for the Aves escaping the chapel adjoining it, the keep was in stillness. I prowled on mice feet, first to the kitchen.

Oh ho!

Here was a fat pig sizzling on its spit. Hoisting my forbidden knife, I was tempted by the crackling skin.

Never play the fool with yourself, my lad.

Mouth already swimming in anticipation, I passed on the delicacy to make inroads on the flesh beneath.

Hot! But done to a turn.

Having dispensed with an Otto-sized portion, I set my sights on the worktables. Bushels of apples lay in wait for roasting. My waistband pocket soon bulged with a fair share—an equal share for Blackspur and me. Pitchers of cream magically lowered themselves by a finger's span each. Cold sliced chicken shared my pouch with dainty meat pies and a loaf from the mound of *pure white* wheaten bread. I thought to add a dollop of freshly churned butter to this abundance but stopped. It was enough. I had no need to add gluttony to my sins.

"Lord Jesus." I raised my eyes not in the direction of the chapel but toward Heaven. "Lord Jesus, I thank you for feeding your poor fool."

I left the scene of my crimes with greater haste than I'd entered it. Yet I did not at once return to the stables. Instead, I climbed the spiral staircase to the room allotted Otto's tame priest. Among all Otto's retainers, Father William was the only one who—like me—could read with facility. On Sundays past, I had made the discovery of the bound manuscripts in this room. Only three, to be sure, but they were wondrous rare. Father William must have pardoned Otto of a monstrous crime to be rewarded with such precious things.

Wiping the last signs of a creamy mustache upon my sleeve, then making certain my fingers were free of grease, I approached with awe the lectern standing in the dim light of a tiny mullioned window. Sitting chained upon it was the Holy Bible. The conceit of using fetters against theft brought a smile. In this entire castle, who but I would covet such a treasure? Taking a deep breath, I spread the heavy leathern covers and chose a page at random.

The Gospel of Saint Matthew.

First I was dazzled by the elegance of the script, then became lost in the Latin my father had been at greater pains to teach me than the tricks of my trade. *Nolite dare sanctum canibus* . . .

> Give not that which is holy unto the dogs, neither cast ye your pearls before swine, lest they trample them under their feet, and turn again and rend you.

A soft whistle escaped my lips. These were the words of the Son of God, truly, but they were also the words of a *man* who had lived as a man—knowing the ways of earthly beasts. Just as I. Why were these words not preached at Sunday Mass? Had I not hidden in the gap behind the chapel's arras often enough to know what was preached— and what not?

The next verse swam before my eyes:

> Ask, and it shall be given you; seek, and ye shall find; knock, and it shall be opened unto you.

Clang . . . Clang . . . Clang . . .

The pealing of the chapel's bell caught me with a start.

Mass was finished too soon. Slamming shut the holy book, I raced for the stairs. Dashed two spirals down. . . . Wait. The chapel doors were creaking open, sending heady incense to fight the reek of the oratory's privy neighbor. I flattened myself next to the hole itself as Otto and his lady paraded by in their Sabbath furs and jewels. Retainers followed, noses righteously in the air. Had they not just watched the Elevation of the Host? Had not the mere seeing of this miracle bettered their chances of salvation?

Why not me, Lord Jesus?

Shrugging off this latest insult to me and my kind, I counted them down to the last and fled. Through the drenching rain to the stables I ran, consoling myself with the letters illuminated in gold and red swimming through my head.

"I've been thinking, Blackspur." We were munching companionably on my trove of apples. I swallowed first and leaned against the wooden stall. "I've been thinking on Lord Jesus's words."

I waited for the horse's nod.

"Well, then, I suspicion that He wasn't only talking about dogs and swine."

A whicker, and Blackspur nudged me for another helping.

"Don't be greedy. It's a nasty trait." Still, I finished my apple to the core and presented him with the remains.

"What I suspicion, my friend, is that He was making a little allegory about mankind."

I reached in my pocket for another apple and crunched into its tang.

"If one were to stretch that to fat Otto—for surely a more swinelike man never existed—what would that be saying about my pearls?"

Blackspur shook his head. But before I could reach the logical conclusion to my learned theory, someone dashed into the stable.

"Conrad!" Christa shook the dripping hood from her head. "His lordship is in a fury because you do not grace his table!"

"By Saint Paul! Time slipped away from me." I yanked my cap tighter, then remembered the state of my motley. "Excuse me, kind dove." I jerked the wool over my head, expecting her to turn a maidenly eye away. She did not.

"You've whip scars all down your back, Conrad!"

"The price of truth." I grinned as my head popped out again. The tunic in its proper place once more, bells jangling from elbows and waist, I gave her a bow.

"Don't sport with me, Conrad. Tonight I'll bring ointments to rub on them."

"Firstly . . ." I reached for her sweet chin and tipped up her delicate face. Too finely boned for a serving wench, it was. Why did I only note that now? Why did it leave me with a curious jolt of surprise? "Firstly, I must live till the night."

✳ ✳ ✳

With great caution, I poked my head into the banqueting hall. Otto was in a rare choler, indeed. In truth, he was in the process of tossing his spiced wine upon the head of his cupbearer.

"Stay!" I cried. "My lord is too profligate! How comes his cupbearer to deserve such honor when his fool be parched?"

Snatching the first three unfilled cups in view, I juggled them through the silenced hall, to the very feet of Otto himself. Then—one, two, three—I brought them back into my keeping to set them in a row upon the dais table. Ruffling my cap's cockscomb, I crowed mightily.

"Hear my plea: one for me, one for thee, and one for the Holy Trinity—since a Sunday after Pentecost it surely be!"

Swooping into a low bow, I held my breath.

It started as a cackle, then grew into huge guffaws. I made bold to glance up. Otto's face was crimson with the effort of his new mirth. Beside him, his lady smiled with relief. Behind me, the hall followed his lead and burst into laughter and applause. Aside me, Till the Cupbearer dared use his towel on his stained face.

"Till!" Otto roared. "More wine! Enough to fill the cup of my good fool thrice—enough to fill the cups of all!"

Another roar, but this of pleasure from the hall. Hot spiced wine rarely made its way south from Lord Otto's dais. I leaped upon the boards to fondle his greasy beard and plant a kiss on his forehead.

"*Tarra-lirra-lee*, great blessings come to thee!"

Then off I scampered before the stinking thick-wit returned to his few senses.

"How like you the blanket I found, Conrad?"

"Exceeding well," I murmured from my prone position upon the extravagant patchwork of softly tanned lambskins Christa had brought me. In my innocence, I never thought to question her saving visit earlier in the day or this lambskin—or yet her newly born interest in this poor jester.

"It beggars belief that you can sleep upon raw straw like an animal. It is hardly fitting—"

"I have hardly been given a choice in the matter. Yet better among the beasts here than among those in the castle's keep."

She sighed, then gently continued rubbing ointments on my stripped back. "Its fleece will warm you in the coming winter, too."

"Will it not be missed?"

"From the bottom of Lord Otto's great sleeping pile? Never!"

"Clever wench. I give thanks it was from the bottom."

She giggled and continued rubbing, though her ointment was gone. Who was I to make protest? Never had I felt so eased, so fine. Why had it taken so long to realize the teasing kitchen girl of my boyhood had grown? Why had Christa taken it upon herself to teach me this truth? *Accept the gift, fool.* I rolled over and reached for her through the darkness.

"And will you not be missed?"

"I fear the spiced wine was so rare to my stomach that the privy called. Another moment must find me well again."

I discovered her lips and stayed her flight an extra second. "Rare wine and rare moments should both be well used."

And so they were.

THREE

I was not always chief (and only) fool to Otto of Schwarzenberg. In better times—if such be not a dream—my father and I wandered the vast lands of the German Empire between village, manor house, and castle, offering our gifts for bed and board. . . .

A clap of thunder sundered the sky, and rain came even heavier. I set down my writing to comfort Blackspur.

"Peace, peace." I rubbed his trembling head and let him bury his mouth against my chest. "If you cannot face Heaven's rumblings with valor, how will you face the thunder of battle?"

He sighed and shook his head loose.

"Yes, I know it has been raining forever. I know you long for exercise. But while this weather holds—" I glanced up toward the rafters at harsher drumbeats. "By Saint Peter! Next Heaven bombards us with hail!"

I sighed, too, then ran a hand along Blackspur's flank.

"While this weather holds, we cannot hunt. Otto is in worse straits than you for lack of it. Even now is he locked in his closet with his bailiff, hearing that his rents will be less because the last of the harvest is ruined. Never mind his poor tenants and serfs, who will find the winter hungrier than usual."

I turned to tuck away my writing tools, then knelt to wrap myself in my lambskin gift against the growing cold seeping through the stables. Cold enough for snow. And when that began, Schwarzenberg would become its own prison. . . .

"It was not so easy on the road, either, Blackspur. I was too young to do more than ape my father's gestures to the crowd. Yet my pratfalls always brought forth a child-hungry woman to share her thin pottage for the night." I stared up the height of my horse. Straight into one eye. "It was early times after the plague. Starving times. Few men for the plowing, few children for the singing . . . When we stumbled onto Otto, it was easier to stay." I smiled. "Then you were born, my friend."

Blackspur had made life bearable from the moment he came forth, like me—ripped from the womb of a dying mother. When Otto's stableman cast him aside with an oath, I gathered the trembling foal to me. It was I who cleaned the afterbirth and set the wobbling creature upon his legs. Begging cows' milk and goats' milk and sheep's milk, I'd suckled him with a bladder till he could crop grass. . . . And so had we grown together, till both were long and strong. Yet his black coat was far sleeker than my tattered motley.

At the crash of another clap of thunder, I shrugged off the warmth of my blanket and rose to groom his coat sleeker still.

Talk of dire omens filled the banqueting hall that night.

"First rains the very like to Noah's flood—"

"Next thunder! And October be upon us!"

From my post straddling the step below Otto's dais, I took in the low murmurs, the bursts of frightened shouts.

"Lightning struck Saint Hedwig's tower bell!"

"Aye—and the sign of Satan was left upon it!"

"Ice from the frozen depths of Hell covers the land!"

Faces buried themselves in ale and more ale till what I feared came at last:

"*Doomsday* is upon us!"

"*Doom . . . Doom . . . Doom . . .*" settled like a sigh through the hall.

Enough.

Springing into a leap, I grabbed the trencher from beneath Otto's very chin. His glazed eyes focused with a snarl.

"You overreach your liberties, fool!"

"Nay, grant me your patience but a moment, good master."

Keeping the plate of hard bread neatly balanced atop my cap, I pranced hither and yon among the lower tables, chanting:

Doom, gloom, soon you'll swoon.
Boom, boom, next the tomb!
But who will feed your lice
Once you've been so neatly iced?

To mutters and scowls of disapproval, I scurried at last to my destination—the frozen courtyard. Piling Otto's platter high with hail, I marched back into the hall, calling: "Steward! A mortar and pestle, if you please! Cook's honey and syrup also seize. A dollop of jam—and *whim-wham zi-ram!* Satan's hail turns into the Grail!"

Johann the Steward stood as frozen as my pile till Otto barked, "For what are you waiting, Steward? For asses' ears to grow upon your head?"

I chuckled as Johann scuttled into action, then paraded with my offering to Otto's table. In a trice, the implements before me, I ground and mixed for my audience of skeptics. Paused for a taste—as any good cook—then added another spoonful of cherry jam.

"Done to a turn!" I grinned and, bowing, presented the mortar bowl to Otto. "Elixir of the gods, my lord, for your delectation."

Otto shoved in his spoon . . . brought it to his mouth . . . gasped.

"Cold!"

Another taste.

"Wondrous!"

Lady Ermengud stretched to poke in her own spoon.

"Oooooh."

She reached for the bowl, but Otto tugged it back. "Make your own Grail Hail!" Then he roared, "*All* may make their own Grail Hail!"

I collapsed onto the step to watch through the flickering torchlight the uproar that followed. Trenchers, broad hats, cloaks—all disappeared with their owners into the dismal night, to return piled high with Satan's (or Heaven's) gift of hail. I pulled out my pipe to add a festive air to the humorous squabbles arising over priority use of the kitchen's supplies. As doom and gloom evaporated with the melting ice, Otto roared again:

"Come to me, my fool of fools!"

With a bow, I piped my way before him.

He shoveled in another spoonful from his fourth helping. Swallowed with a grimace between pain and ecstasy. "A gift I would bestow on you for this most clever of jests! Only ask . . ."

Ask, and it shall be given you. . . .

Another swooping bow brought my eyes to my boots. More specifically, to the toes wrapped in straw poking forth from them. I rose with a grin. "Boots, my lord—so fine and supple, that I need no more to scrape and shuffle." Before he could consider the matter closed, I quickly added, "And a cloak to keep me safe and warm through all long winter's heavy storms."

He hiccuped and shoved his spoon back into his ice. "Both shall be yours!"

I salaamed my way from the dais till I backed into Fang and his fellows. "Avaunt, ye curs!" I cried. Clutching a well-chewed thighbone, I thrust it toward the rafters. "This night is mine!"

Above me, Otto smacked his hands red. Around me, the hall resounded in stamps and cheers.

"How do you think of such things, Conrad?"

Christa had made use of the general tumult to slip out of the hall after me. We hid behind the staircase, stealing warmth from each other's arms.

"If I knew, I would be jester to the emperor himself, not fat Otto." I nuzzled her neck. She smelled much better than Blackspur. "Common sense, my father would say. Seeing a need and addressing it with all one's wits."

"Hailstorms will never be the same in Schwarzenberg," she murmured.

"All to the good. Would I were wise enough to banish the coming winter."

Christa stretched up for my lips. "Love can melt even the snows."

Her kiss was almost proof enough. I pulled away with reluctance. This new Christa was fast shackling my very soul. "Off with you, sparrow, lest you tempt us both to Hell."

"Where it is at least warm." Then she made a quick sign of the cross and kissed the Agnus Dei medallion around her neck for good measure. "Forgive me, Conrad. I cannot explain my feelings for you any more than you can explain your jests. Yet I have been watching you these long ten years. Watching and waiting—"

"Catch a chill and all that effort will have been in vain." I led her back to the great hall's door. "Get you to your bed!"

Sweet Christa stuck out her tongue, but obeyed. All that remained was for me to reel across the courtyard's icy battlefield. I laughed as my toes scraped against the rough missiles.

Ask, and it shall be given you.

Soon I would be properly shod. Properly warmed. What came next?

Seek, and ye shall find.

My quest would require more thought.

 # FOUR

*Some among the nobility have always favored the
natural fool—he of the humped back, dwarfed
body, and dwarfed mind. The more enlightened of
rulers understands the usefulness of the artificial
fool. Who but such has complete access to his
lord's ear? Who but such may criticize the folly of
the times with impunity? For has he not o'ertaken
the natural fool's innocent access to God's ear—
and turned this conceit into truth-telling?*

Such musings I scribbled after Otto's latest attack of
imbecility. Fortunately, this eruption occurred *after* I
came into possession of my new fitted boots and
warm felt cloak.

"Will you never learn, Conrad?"

Christa was rubbing fresh ointments onto the fresh
welts embellishing my beleaguered back.

"Nay," I groaned, "not till Otto be taught to think."

"But he *cannot* be taught to think!"

"Pearls before swine," I muttered.

"What's that?"

"Nothing, my thrush. . . . Ouch! Take a care!"

"I should have applied a plaster first. Mayhap it's not too late to beg Cook to concoct one—"

"Don't leave!" I begged.

"Have it your way." Her touch became more gentle still. "But whatever possessed you to intervene on behalf of Jurgen the Bailiff? He who's never done you a good deed—"

"Never forget the serfs, Christa."

"By the Holy Virgin, Conrad. And now you take on the woes of the entire world?"

"Who else will speak for the serfs? Did they deserve to be flogged because they could not pay their rents to Otto? Did Jurgen deserve to be publicly flogged for not collecting what does not exist?"

"So you present yourself as a scapegoat for all of them?"

"Nay, I merely whispered in dim Otto's ear that crops may come again with the spring—a merciful God willing—but where was he to find another bailiff after humiliating and exiling Jurgen? And for that matter, who might plow and harrow his fields at the wished-for spring with half the able men of the village crippled by his hundred blows?"

Beneath the waves of fever heat pulsing through my spine, I turned my mind once more to the afternoon's events. The courtyard spread before me: Otto holding forth, whip in hand, from the keep's steps; retainers to each side, sticks and their own whips to the ready . . . though their faces bore signs of reluctance. Not for the punishment they'd lustily mete out but from the thought of Otto's turning next on *them*. And facing these, Jurgen the Bailiff and his cowering debtors. Thankfully, the scene faded before I was divested of my cloak and tunic, before I need relive the fury of the blows against my bowed but steady body. My wry smile was lost to the darkness.

"Ah, Christa, perhaps my fault lay in speaking the truth unadorned by rhyme or foolery. Who else was Otto to lay his wrath upon, with his chosen victims pardoned?"

The next shudder running through my body brought the long-buried reality to the fore.

"In God's truth," I murmured, "Otto is not numbered among the enlightened rulers of this world. Better I'd been a dwarf drooling like his hounds."

Christa's sigh evaporated with the onset of stealthy footsteps through the darkness. I bolted half up, then wished I hadn't. "Who goes there?"

"Be not afeard, good fool, sir."

A ragged man-shape materialized, pulling a hidden lantern from beneath his coverings. Its faint light illuminated a rough face and matted hair.

"I be Martin from the village, sir." A nod to me, a second recognizing Christa. "A simple plowman and serf. I bear succor from the goodwives." Pots emerged from hidden pouches. "A healing broth filled with herbs, and plasters for your back. Good plasters, sir. Our wives be knowing in the ways of curing the whip's taste. They be having much practice."

"Oh, thank you!" Christa cried before I had the opportunity. She snatched the offerings, shoved me flat again, and began administering the cure.

"That be all." Martin bobbed. "I must away before the bells ring compline. Before the castle gate be locked. May God and his saints send blessings upon you for taking our part!"

Hiding his light, Martin the Plowman disappeared.

"And what say you to that"—I twisted my head up— "little sparrow?"

"Don't move! The plasters must stiffen!"

Another set of footsteps broke the night's cold stillness. This set crunched with authority across the courtyard. I felt Christa's hands tense, then heard her scuttle off into hiding somewhere in the stalls beyond. A flaming torch that sent Blackspur into a neigh of fear introduced the bailiff's servant Karl. He flung down an armload of clothing, then tossed a small purse atop it.

"Greetings from my master, fool. With all the blood you shed at nones time, he thought you might need these." With a wrinkle of his nose, Karl about-faced and strode from the stables.

"Is he gone?" Christa's whisper came through a gap between the slats behind me.

"Quite. And his arrogance with him."

She slipped back to examine my new bounty as best as

possible. Cloth shook ghostlike in the air. "I think it's a shirt, Conrad!"

"Good. The first since I grew from out my last a full two years past. It will ease the scrape of tunic's wool against my back."

She waved something else white. And giggled. "Braies! One, no . . . two sets!"

"Better still. Underwear is hard found. One can scarcely ask it for a boon."

A snicker, followed by a jingling. "No words of thanks from the mighty bailiff, but he sends coins, too."

"Bite them for me, to make certain they be real."

"The man has no cause to add insult to injury. Still . . ." Silence, then, "They are real enough, Conrad. There might even be gold!"

"The best yet. May I move now? I have need for that soup before it turns stone cold. The sooner I heal, the sooner I can begin saving my pearls."

"What are you talking about?" She worried over strapping the plasters in place, helped me sit, then pulled my wooden spoon from my waistband and began ladling soup into my mouth.

"I believe I have found"—a pause to swallow—"my true quest at last."

"A quest? As in your tales of Roland or Arthur?"

"Pray God not quite so epic."

"*What*, Conrad?"

I made attempt to square my shoulders nobly . . . an

ill-thought gesture. But when the moan passed, my voice was as strong as my intent. The afternoon's lessons had been more than painful. They'd taught me that I might not survive another such tutelage—and Otto's choleric nature being what it was, more lessons were sure to follow.

"I shall quest for a new master. An *enlightened* new master."

The spoon slipped from her hand with a dull thud. Christa was nobody's fool and never would be.

"You would *leave*."

"With pleasure. Leave Otto the imbecile. Leave Schwarzenberg the cold and heartless—"

"Leave *me?*" she breathed. "Now? Just as we've begun?"

I grabbed for the bowl and drank it down. "I will return for you, sweet dove—"

"The way men return from war? Never?"

"Little sparrow—"

She yanked the pot from my grip and flung it at the nearest wall. Thankfully, it was of sturdy peasant crafting and survived, as peasants usually do.

"Enough of your honeyed words. *Little sparrow, sweet dove, thrush,*" she spat. "I am not like the others. Where go my favors goes my heart—forever on this earth, and into eternity beyond. You'll not be leaving me behind, Conrad!"

I threw up my arms in defense against her words, only to groan again at the rekindled pain. "Be reasonable, girl!"

"*Woman!* Am I not of marriageable age?" she near shouted. "Have I not the same years as you?"

"Be reasonable, woman," I amended. "How can I carry you with me? How can I care for you on the long road?"

She reached for my arms, grasped my hands. "I will sleep on straw. I will sleep on dirt. I will sleep on snow—so long as I rest beside you."

"But—"

My wild bird had not finished.

"I will grovel for bones among hounds, so long as I take my meat with you. I will—"

I silenced her lips with mine. How could love be fairer said? And yet—

I pulled away. "I am a jester. I own nothing but my bells and my wit. I have no sword to defend you. And one as lovely as you will need defense."

Christa slowly rose. Had the darkness been not so heavy, I could have sworn it was with the dignity of a queen.

"Think well on your words, Conrad. Think well on mine. For now, I bid you a good night."

A good night? With the fever upon me? With her parting words more painful than my scarred back? *Mercy.* I took a deep breath preparatory to unburdening my woes to the nodding Blackspur. Exhaled it with a chuff when Christa called back, "In Heaven's name, have the common sense to wrap your blanket about you, foolish Conrad!"

Grinning, I did my sparrow's bidding. Next to me, Blackspur stamped a hoof and sniffed as if to say, "At last! A little peace!"

FIVE

My father could sing songs of courtly love in French and German both, though they always sounded sweeter in French. His voice was rich, yet subtle for such a bear of a man. Alas, he did not bequeath this voice to me. But he did bequeath his trove of epic tales, fabliaux . . . and, most especially, the poems of the troubadours—

I set down my quill with a groan. The night had not been good. It had been long. Long, and filled with thoughts I would rather not address. As the matins bells of midnight blended into lauds, then the prime bells of dawn, none of the peals brought relief. My usually lithe body was frozen in stiff aches—leaving only my fingers fit to write, only my mind fit to wander in maddening circles. I sighed, stared up at Blackspur, and surrendering to my melancholy humor, recited from the very depths of my soul:

All self-command is now gone by,
E'er since the luckless hour when she
Became a mirror to my eye. . . .
Thou fatal mirror! There I spy
Love's image; and my doom shall be . . .
To sigh, and thus expire, beholding thee!

Blackspur snorted contempt.

"As well you may, my friend. Why has that wench, that *woman*, chosen to bewitch me in such an ill-timed fashion? Go I must. Take her with me I cannot. Surely you can comprehend the nature of my trials—"

"In faith, Conrad, you talk to your horse as if he can understand!"

I waited for my jarred heartbeat to still. Had she overheard some? All? "Of course he can."

Fair Christa snorted her own snort and slung something at me.

"Your breakfast."

"Many thanks—"

"Save your thanks and breakfast both. Let me see to your wounds. I'm wanted back in the kitchen."

Setting aside the napkin of bread and cheese, I lay down and prepared to surrender to those loving fingers. . . . "*Ouch!*"

"The plasters had need to come off."

"But half my back with them?"

In answer, cold ointments met raw skin.

"*Christ's wounds!*"

"Save your blasphemy, too. Only see you let the ointments dry before rising."

"Christa! Sparrow!"

She was gone.

I creaked my neck toward Blackspur above. "How could one so loving but the night before turn so heartless with the coming dawn?" I shivered a shiver that played its way down my frigidly anointed spine. "And yet another riddle: How comes this ice to burn a deeper hole within me than all my lady's former cosseting?"

Ignoring Blackspur's total disdain, I retreated yet again to the wisdom of the troubadours:

> *Love acts like the spark*
> *From the embers under the ashes*
> *Which fires the wood and burns the house*
> *—Listen!—*
> *And one does not know where to flee*
> *When one is burnt by this fire.*

Abandoned by all, I sank with a will into my misery.

And so I sighed and moaned and healed. Christa remained as curt and cold as the coming winter on her brief visits of mercy. The second day she spoke but one sentence: "When do you leave?"

My answer was as short. "When strong enough to ride Blackspur."

She did not question my taking Blackspur. Should she have, I was prepared with a thousand reasons. Had Otto's man not cast the foal aside at his birth? Had I not nursed him into life and health? Would Blackspur allow any other upon his back? My justifications could be tallied to infinity and back again. Yet only one counted. He was more than confidant, more than my only family. Blackspur was half of me. Never could I leave him behind—even knowing the taking would be cried *theft*. Even knowing Otto was like to harry me to kingdom come for the act.

The fifth day found me practicing the morning exercises my father had laid upon me.

"Each new dawn, Conrad. Without fail. Allow your muscles and limbs to grow idle, and your strength will disappear. With it goes your wit—and your supper. What master listens to a fool who cannot dance rings around him?"

Up among the rafters with the stable swallows, I swung by two hands, then glanced down at my horse. "Almost there, Blackspur. We must be gone before the snow. Before being trapped with mad Otto for another endless winter." I let go to bounce onto the straw. "Yet I think it behooves me to steal one more day of leisure."

So saying, I reached in my pouch for my three balls of stitched leather and set myself to while away the hours in juggling and thought.

"Otto calls for you, Conrad!"

Christa appeared with the ringing of the vespers bells.

"Does he?"

"Ranting at your absence," she continued, "as if the fault were your own."

I shrugged off my lambskin and rose. "I'd best attend him, then."

I did not call her *sparrow* or *thrush* or *dove*. She did not offer her lips. Cloaked in the weighty silence between us, we went at Otto's bidding to attend to Otto's pleasures.

I danced and made music. I pranced and made jokes. I fawned when Otto looked upon me. One thing I would not do.

Otto burped and shoved away from his table. "Well played, fool. We are pleased. You may be excused to your supper."

A jingling, swooping bow. "With thanks, good master. Yet days in pain have changed my needs—I fain would sup with greater ease. Heed me, if you please. I shall swallow where your courtiers wallow!"

A handspring brought me to the nearest table. I reached for an idle cup of ale, for the near-empty bowl of meat—

"You try me, fool!" Otto bellowed.

I thrust out my tongue as if to taste . . . made a gagging sound and a wretched face. "Nay, good master! Thanks all the same. My taste is not for you, but for this goodly pot of stew!"

Rumblings surrounded me as the hall attempted mightily to hide chuckles, and worse. On the dais above, Lady Ermengud covered her mouth with a protective hand, yet her eyes cried laughter. Otto grew crimson, then purple, then managed to strangle out, "Well jested. We give you grace of the boards this night."

In answer, I shoved his closest retainer for room upon the bench and fell to with the pot of stew.

I was packed by the lauds bells.

"Three of the morning," I murmured to Blackspur as I woke him for an extra feed. "Eat well, my friend. More oats may be long in coming."

As he munched his windfall, I groomed him in the dark. I knew his shape so well—every swirl in his black coat, every hair upon his mane and tail—that the undertaking was simple. The same with his bridle and saddle. For adding my sleeping pack of lambskin and all else hidden within, I chanced striking flint to the stable lantern. By its light, I quickly accomplished the last. Next I need only wait for dawn, the prime bells, and the opening of the castle gate. I blew out the light.

"Pray with me, Blackspur. Pray to good Saint Francis, who loved all creatures great and small. Pray our escape be good. Pray my quest be not in vain." I paused as he bobbed his head beneath my hand. "Pray I choose well in leaving love behind."

In the end, I could not wait for the bells. My near-cracked heart bid instant escape. Blackspur's iron shoes wrapped in rags against their clatter, I led him toward the gate. Faint rose touched edges of the sky as belated peals sounded from the chapel behind me. Beyond the castle walls, the chimes of Saint Hedwig's joined in. From an alcove next to the gate, a cowled servant began grinding the wheels that would raise the portcullis to freedom beyond. I thought not why I wasn't hailed. My eyes were only for the expanding vista: the plateau spreading below the looming castle, and winding through it—the road. Slipping under the grille's sharp iron points, I tugged Blackspur forth and mounted him. He neighed with excitement.

"Hush. Let the world sleep a little later this day." I tightened my hand on the reins and made ready to nudge him onward—

Something—someone—darted before us . . . halted midway on the drawbridge. Blocked my path to freedom.

"Out of the way!" I cried. "In God's name. In God's mercy!"

The hood was cast off. "Has the sun risen high enough to blind you, Conrad?"

I leaned forward. Surely it was Christa's voice. Yet . . . I looked upon a lad. A very fair and well-appointed lad.

"I swear I'll be no trouble! On all the saints will I swear it!"

"Christa! Your clothing! Your hair! What have you done to your hair?"

She tossed her head. Her locks were golden still, though cropped near as short as mine. "Is it not easier to defend a lad than a lady?"

"Sparrow—"

"And I can sing, Conrad. Did you know that I can sing?"

As to trouble, I was staring deep into its blue eyes. But, hey-ho, if she could *sing* . . .

My heart rising with the dawn, I reached for her. "Up quickly then, my songbird. Blackspur has strength enough to carry both."

She came to me.

SIX

Were I a rich lord, I would bestow half my fortune in gratitude for this day. Nay, not wasted on a pardoner in exchange for useless indulgences. What need I for ten thousand years' reprieve from Purgatory? Squander it on Masses to free my soul from the everlasting flames of Hell? Never. Were not Purgatory and Hell already here on earth? Mayhap Heaven, too . . . Enough. I would make my bequest to serfs that they might buy their freedom—and in breaking their bonds look upon the world with new eyes. As I now do. Verily, the Wheel of Fortune spins my way.

The road through Schwarzenberg goes but north or south. Since nothing lay north save more cold, I turned Blackspur toward the south. As if celebrating our freedom, the rising sun gifted us with a last burst of warmth. Past Otto's open fields, and into the safety of the great forests of birch and fir beyond, we cantered. I flung off my hood, then tugged off my jester's cap. A fresh breeze caressed my liberated head—

"Conrad! Never have I seen your hair in the sunshine. It is red!"

I let loose a roar of pure pleasure. "Aye, and I think I shall let it grow. Let it curl to my shoulders—nay, even to my toes!"

"Then who will wear your belled cap?"

Grinning, I tightened Christa's hold around my waist. "*You* may, if you dare!"

She laughed. "The foolery may come later. For now, you'd best teach me songs to sing."

"At once?"

"At once!"

More prodding I did not need. Was it not a day destined for making music? And had I not the perfect song for my nightingale? "I give you, then, a lied of our own minnesingers, 'Unter den Linden.' It is the equal to any of the troubadours' verses." And so I recited:

> *Under the linden,*
> *On the heather,*
> *For us two a bed there was;*
> *There you could see,*
> *Entwined together,*
> *Broken flowers and bruised grass,*
> *From a thicket in the dale—*

Tandaradei!—
Sweetly sang the nightingale.

I felt my Christa's blush as she laid her face against my neck. "I fear . . . oh, Conrad, I fear my advances were . . . were *in advance of* experience. . . ."

I turned to her. "All the better. We will learn love's ways together. But not till the time be ripe. For now, prove you did not magnify your other graces. I wait to hear you sing, my bird."

She stiffened righteously. "Give me but the tune."

Slowing Blackspur, I fetched pipe from pouch. "*Under the linden*, like so." From habit, I worked the finger stops and trilled the notes. "*On the heather, / For us two a bed there was* . . ."

Christa sang. Like a nightingale she sang. Pure . . . nigh *holy*, the notes filled the bluing sky. Blackspur pricked his ears and neighed his approval. Joyfully pulling pipe from lips, I near upset us all in attempting to properly show my own approval.

"You can *sing*."

"Did I not swear? Back to your pipe, Conrad. I need to know the rest of the song. I need to know *many* songs. I'll not be left behind when you find your new master!"

"Never!" And I broke into the second verse:

> *I sped thither*
> *Through the glade;*

My love had reached the spot before.
There was I snared,
Most happy maid! . . .
Many a time he kissed me there—
Tandaradei!
See my lips, how red they are!

The narrow dirt road wended for hours between forested hills and scattered villages deserted since the plague times, wildness already overtaking their fallow fields. Seeing the huts with their roofs sagging into smokeless chimneys—no sound of crying babes or gently nagging mothers coming through the open doors; huts abandoned even by nesting birds—I murmured a prayer for my mother and those who had joined her. But I was not unhappy with the empty highway. There'd be none to say our passing, should Otto pursue.

The sun was at its zenith when Blackspur's pace slowed to a walk.

"Enough for now, my friend." Leaning to pat his neck, I eased down to the dusty road. I smiled at Christa, still enthroned. "He needs to rest, and so do we."

She slumped into my arms with a groan—then a greater one as she touched the ground and stretched her body. "Oh! I may be crippled for life!"

"Only sore a few days till you find your seat."

"I know already where is my *seat*," she complained, "and wish further riding could be upon my head!"

I laughed and guided both along a stream, deep into the

protection of the forest. "Here is our glade. Rest you on the heather, my nightingale, while I tend to Blackspur."

So I led my horse to water, then knelt beside him for my own drink. But Christa did not rest upon the heather. Instead, she crept behind me and most villainously shoved—

"What—" I pulled my dripping head from the icy water. "*What* in Heaven's name—"

"In Heaven's name," she answered, "I would wash your hair!"

From nowhere came a hard lump of soap, followed by much scrubbing. Too much scrubbing. A final dunk—

I came up spluttering. "Are you satisfied, woman?"

She handed me a shirt as towel. "I would the rest of you were scrubbed as well, but that must wait for warmer waters."

"Saints be praised for small mercies." Shivering, I reached for the comfort of my cap.

"Nay!"

Out of my fingers it was snatched. In horror, I watched Christa lay water and lye soap upon *my very identity*. "It could shrink!" I yelped.

"More like expand, with all the vermin gone," she calmly replied, bashing it against a rock like a common washerwoman.

"The bells may rust!"

"Giving the alchemists a new wonder to ponder, for never have I seen brass go to rust."

"Blackspur!" I cried. "Put a stop to this nonsense!"

More wise than I, Blackspur chose neutrality. Serenely

ambling to an unsullied stretch of water, he continued his drink. I set to with rubbing feeling back into my benumbed skull till Christa stiffened.

"What now?" I complained.

"Hush. The road."

I paused to listen. Blackspur raised his dripping mouth and flicked his ears.

Hoofbeats.

"Don't move!" I ordered both.

Flinging aside my towel, I wove with stealth through the thick woods till nigh upon the road. With a spring, I scaled the limbs of a ponderous dark fir. In but another moment was I settled within its sheltering boughs. Only just in time. Surging hell-bent over the highway came Lord Otto himself and all his retainers—on the hunt. For me! Subtlety never Otto's strength, he missed the signs of where we'd left the road. Signs I'd not again err in leaving: Blackspur's iron hoofprints veering from the dusty path; hoofprints following the stream itself—a goodly stream, with water clean enough for any thirsty horse.

"Onward!" Otto bellowed through the drumming hooves. "The knave and my horse cannot be far beyond!" From the rear of his hard-ridden palfrey, his next words returned to me. "*I* must seize the brazen thief! . . . *I* must choose the tree and limb upon which he is to be hanged! . . . And the trollop, too!"

Grasping my very clean neck, I gulped. Only letting go of neck and tree when the haze of the party had settled, I scampered to the road to make certain Blackspur's passing was obliterated.

Hah. The numbskulls did my work for me, crushing our signs into the dirt.

Whistling bravely, I returned to our secret bower, eliminating the marks along the stream for good measure. "An extended meal might be called for, sparrow."

"Extended till Otto tires of the chase and is safely away to his castle again?"

"You heard?"

"Lord Otto's roar could beggar any bull's."

I tugged my dripping cap from out her grip and laid it in a patch of sun. Next I took her in my arms. She trembled like a caged bird. "And is there aught to feast upon?"

"No thanks to you, Sir Head in the Clouds Fool!"

Fear was replaced with bread and hard sausage. We nibbled till the hunting party limped past on its return journey. Christa was still pale.

"Why did he hunt without his hounds, Conrad?"

I'd been considering the same question. The hounds would have made short work of us, getting their revenge for too many nights of contested suppers. "The way was long. . . . He chose speed."

Christa made the sign of the cross. "Thank the good God and the Holy Virgin—"

"And all the saints!" I added with fervor. Then I strained my neck to examine the patch of sky above. "There remains but an hour or two before vespers and dusk . . . yet I think more distance would not go amiss. . . ."

Christa was already collecting the remains of our meal. "Nay. Not at all."

Knowing Otto wasn't bright enough to leave a straggling spy, I chanced cheering our spirits. I began singing the last verse of "Unter den Linden" as I made Blackspur ready.

> *How shamed were I*
> *If anyone*
> *(Now Heaven forfend!) had there been*
>   *nigh—*

"Pray, Conrad," Christa cried, "stop! Your voice is an abomination! Like to . . . like to a snaggletoothed saw cutting through the notes!"

Grinning hugely, I soldiered on:

> *There we two lay,*
> *But that was known*
> *To none except my love and I,*
> *And the little nightingale—*

Christa attacked with the jangling bells of my damp cap.

> *Who, I know, will tell no tale.*

Too late, her lips stilled mine.

And so the waning day spread its last glories before us. Otto's wrath lay behind. Ahead, our future beckoned.

We were blessed with a clear night. By the light of the moon, I urged Blackspur on. Still, I felt the cold gathering. When the next stream crossed our path, I led my horse into it, and so we followed the water till the forest enclosed us.

"Here." I swung down and reached for Christa. "I'd hoped for better shelter, but this must do for tonight."

Thus we set up camp. And when all was snug, I felt the call of my quill and ink. . . .

"Do you write every day, Conrad?"

I set my inkpot next to the fire lest it freeze in the night. "Only when I have something to say."

Christa inspected our meal, impaled on sticks over the flames. "Will you teach me to read? Like a true lady?"

I reached to hug her. "You are a truer lady than Ermengud herself. But, yes, I will teach you."

"When?"

"Will it keep till we sup? I confess to a mighty hunger, and there's nary hound to fight nor bone to gnaw in sight."

Her laughter flowed over me like a soft spring breeze, banishing the night's chill. Then we supped on toasted bread and cheese. Later, her head upon my lap within our lambskin cocoon, I began explaining the alphabet—till Christa *yawned.*

"You lied, wench," I whispered. "You have no interest in the letters!"

"Truly, I do, only . . . I sat up half the night plying Rupert the Gatekeeper with stolen wine, then battling his advances till he fell flat upon his ugly face—"

"How did you know?" I interrupted. "How could you know this was to be the day?"

"Silly fool," she murmured. "After your refusal to dine among Otto's hounds? Anyone who knew you could tell that was nigh to flinging down a gauntlet before him. Fortunately, none knew you so well as I."

The brazen hussy flapped her lashes at me.

"Next," she blithely continued, "it was necessary to tend to my new coiffure." She smiled into my eyes. "How do you find it, Conrad?"

I caressed her golden curls. "Devilish handsome. I'll be fighting off the maidens till they think we two have a forbidden love."

She giggled. "Something you'd not thought on when you refused my joining you."

"Indeed not."

"After accomplishing all of that," she resumed, "I had to float through the keep like a wraith, stealing the most becoming—and cleanest—wardrobe for my new role." Another yawn. "Finally, I was obliged to raid the kitchen for provisions, since I knew you'd never consider your stomach."

I tickled her. "I am but a thing of air and light. Insubstantial—"

"And, without a little looking after, like to dissolve into air and light before you solve your quest."

"It was excellent toasted cheese. Thank you, my dove."

"You are welcome." Her eyes closed.

Bending, I placed a kiss on each lid. "And will you not miss the castle? Miss Schwarzenberg?"

I thought she'd neither the strength nor the passion remaining for the vehemence of her sudden answer.

"My parents sold me into service when I was but five, the better to feed their other hungry mouths. And after Lord Otto's decree? I mourn *no one*."

I hugged her to me till she did sleep. Then I rose to throw more wood upon the fire and check my horse. He nodded where the moon's silver beams broke through the forest canopy. Now its face was wreathed by a halo of clouds. *Snow signs.*

"Blackspur"—I rubbed his neck—"keep watch for me this night. I am past weary and fain must rest."

My faithful friend shook sleep from his head and softly nickered me back to my bed.

SEVEN

The second volume of Father William's small library had been Vincent de Beauvais's collection of all knowledge, the Speculum. *In it, Vincent called woman "the confusion of man, an insatiable beast, a continuous anxiety, an incessant warfare, a daily ruin, a house of temper, a hindrance to devotion." A fine memory being necessary to my calling, I could not help but remember those words . . . and others. Others claiming woman's counsel lost Paradise to Adam. But was not Adam given the same free will as Eve? Was not Adam able to think—able to choose between good and evil? More: Had not God Almighty Himself said it was not good for man to be alone? And had not my father honored the memory of my mother's excellence—and loved none other till his dying day?*

"**O**h!"

Christa's sharp cry woke me with a start. "What troubles you?"

She burrowed deeper into my protective arm. "I dreamed it was Friday. And it *must* be Friday, for surely yesterday was Thursday—"

Befuddled by sleep, I grasped for the nature of her worry. "And so?"

"We have no fish for the fast day!"

"Ho!" I snorted. "Silly chick." I twisted to tweak her nose. "Never eating a good meal's meat in a year, how can I be enjoined to fast?"

Christa played with a pout. "That may be all very well for you, but how am I to be dispensed?"

"Easily, sparrow." I placed a kiss upon her head next her brow, to calm her ruffled feathers. "Are not armies on the march dispensed from fasting? And are we not marching as to war in our noble quest?"

Her lips curled into the beginnings of a smile. "You argue much better than Father William ever did, Conrad, though I suspect a fallacy somewhere. . . ."

I eased my numb arm from beneath her and shook some life into it, then lifted a flap of our lambskin tent. "No matter. None at all. Our first battle is upon us."

Christa lunged for me. "Otto?" she gasped. "A Free Company of raiders?"

"Neither." I widened the gap so she could see for herself. "Our battle will be with Nature."

"Snow!"

I shook the accumulation from over our heads and peered through the sheet still falling with a vengeance. "Pray Lord Jesus's mercy. Winter has found us."

Blackspur was strong as any warhorse. On a good travel day with dry roads—even with Christa's extra weight upon his broad back—he could take us twenty-five miles. Twenty-five miles farther from Otto and Schwarzenberg. Twenty-five miles closer to the attainment of my goal.

It was not a good travel day.

I hunched over Blackspur's neck to brush ice from his eyes. "Just a little more, my friend. Take us just a little farther, till shelter be found."

He shook his great head and plunged forward into the snow. For each step, he must raise his forelegs higher above the accumulation. One foot? . . . In some places, two feet. The road had long since been hidden from view. We traveled now through a tunnel of fir trees, their limbs bowed by the weight of the first snow. Above us, rare glimpses of the sky showed it whitened out by the deluge still dropping from the heavens. Thus had we been riding since Christa and I had hastily broken camp. How many hours? I'd lost the very feel for passing time.

"Conrad?"

Christa thrust a fist at me. I grasped for her frozen fingers, tried to impart some nonexistent warmth from my own. For all these hours, she had been my tower of strength—singing through the tempest till her voice be near lost, rousing me with hugs when I slumped in exhaustion. "Sparrow?"

"Take this, please. You need strength."

I bit into the hard end of a sausage. Laughed. "And is it still Friday?"

"I'm sure I cannot tell. But since this is all the food we possess . . ."

I chewed carefully, swallowed my bite, and passed back the remains. "Your share."

"But, Conrad—"

"Don't argue." The latest gust of frigid wind near stole my words away. "While yet of this earth, we share all."

"Even hunger?"

"Especially that."

Cold, too. Perhaps death. The bit of food gave me power enough to set my mind to that thought. . . . Little matter my unbaptized state. My conscience was at ease. Had not honorable men lived before Christ's First Coming? Would not they, too, arise on the Day of Judgment, when Jesus Christ Himself performed the Harrowing of Hell? . . . Verily, death would not be a terror with soul at rest—and my snowbird to share it. And she would have her wish to lie beside me in the snow as it slowly stole our last warmth—

"Conrad!"

I jerked from my melancholy thoughts.

"Look!"

Brushing ice from my own lashes, I looked. Was it possible? Our shrouded tunnel was widening. I kicked Blackspur's sides, and he strained harder. Whitened mounds emerged from a clearing within the trees. Walls . . . buildings. Before them all spread the arms of a cross, Christ's stone figure crucified upon it in snow.

A *monastery!* There was no monastery so rich, none so poor, as did not keep a guesthouse for weary travelers.

"Thank you, Lord Jesus," slipped through my cracked lips. "For death, later be always better than sooner."

Blackspur did not need another nudge. With a prodigious neigh, he strove straight for the gate.

Knock, and it shall be opened unto you.

In lieu of a knocker was a bell pull—near frozen into the wood of the gate. Wresting it free, I yanked with a will. Waited. Yanked again. Waited not so long before my next attack—

"Who goes there?"

"In God's name, pilgrims."

Too slowly, the gate creaked open. A squat robed figure barred our way, squinting suspiciously from beneath his cowl: at me, at Blackspur, at Christa still upon his back. "It is past the season for pilgrimage, and what pilgrim is rich enough to travel by horse?"

I held myself firmly planted before him yet lowered my hooded head in obeisance. "Are we not all pilgrims on the road of life? All pilgrims in search of Heaven?" With that, I shook my head—and the hidden bells of my cap, which I'd thought long since frozen into silence, jingled. Before my eyes, the monk's dark scowl turned into a broad smile.

"You are an entertainer!"

I bowed as elegantly as possible within the drifted snow near reaching my thighs. "But a poor jester, Brother. At your service." I nodded toward Christa. "And my apprentice."

"Come in, come in!" He waved us forward. "Out of the weather, in God's name. You are welcome with joy to lighten the storm for my brothers and me!"

"And my horse?"

"The best of oats await him in our stable!"

Thus this unbaptized fool and his lady in disguise entered not the guesthouse—but the very inner sanctum of a celibate monastery.

EIGHT

The whole of Christendom knows that Saint Bruno cleansed monastery life with his founding of the ascetic Order of Carthusians three hundred years past. Next, Saint Bernard of Clairvaux purified the Cistercians. Yet what had these holy hermits to do with the common man? It was only Saint Francis of Assisi and his Little Brothers who dared open their eyes to the poor and suffering among us. It was only they who chose to walk in sandals like Lord Jesus, in the steps of Lord Jesus, begging their bread in poverty and succoring all. Yet time and Holy Mother Church have a way of shifting the best of intentions. . . .

Christa got her Friday fish after all. For that matter, so did I. But this only after our sodden garments had been exchanged for the warm, long robes of Franciscan novices. Only after we had separately enjoyed the heated waters of the monastery's bathing room. Only after I had braved the storm again in search of Blackspur, to find he'd been dried and groomed and fed in a stall that beggared in opulence any comparison to his old home in Otto's domain.

"The codfish stew was very fine," Christa murmured in my ear at table. "Nicely peppered, with all that heavy cream . . ."

"The *white* bread and fresh salted butter even finer," I answered.

Brother Sebastian—for he it was who'd greeted us at the gate—shoved a bowl from across the boards. "Never neglect our apples. Baked with sugar and cinnamon and cloves!" A wooden tray followed. "And the pride of Brother Anselm— our own cheeses." He stabbed at a round with his knife. "Hard cow cheese, and soft goat cheese, and a most goodly sheep cheese betwixt and between."

At which profligacy, I fear my discretion fled completely. "Cream . . . rare sugar, rarer spices," I exclaimed. "For a mendicant order, you monks eat like princes!"

The good brother laughed, setting his extra chins to wobbling. "Do you take up your dispute with the wealthy who bequeath us winter comforts in hopes of saving their worldly souls. Come spring, we will take to the preaching roads refreshed—and our begging bowls empty of all save offered pottage once more."

I shrugged and reached for the cheese. "In that case, many thanks—"

"Nay, it is we who must thank you, for when you've filled

your stomachs, you must fill our hearts with delight. Only think how they sank with the first snow arriving at lauds . . . growing heavier still at our prime devotions. Without your coming, by vespers there would have been no contact with the outside world, no escape from each other till spring."

Another, much younger friar hurried over to whisper in Sebastian's ear. He bobbed his tonsured gray head with enthusiasm, then turned to me. "Now, Conrad, you and your assistant—"

"Christ-Christof," I managed to stammer.

Brother Sebastian beamed. "You and Christof must go with Brother John. He has prepared your costumes for your performance."

Indeed, Brother John had. In a nearby chamber was laid out all of our clothing, clean and pressed dry. I picked up my fool's cap. Its bells shone with polishing. "My thanks, Brother."

He nodded acceptance. "Saint Francis believed in the joyful life." Then he waited—obviously for us to make the change of garments.

I glanced at Christa and saw true terror cross her face. "If you would excuse us but a moment, Brother? Christof is yet a modest youth—"

"A thousand pardons!"

As his sandals scraped out, I listened for the scufflings to disappear down the slate-paved corridor. Next I firmly shut the heavy wooden door. Turned to Christa. "Safe!"

"Thank the Virgin! Help me out of this heavy robe, Conrad. But close your eyes?" she pleaded.

"Anything, my dove."

She loosened the girdle rope, and we both yanked. Yet the rough wool brushed my eyes open—

"What have you wound yourself with?"

"I am a woman, Conrad. To conceal that little fact requires a breast band. Besides, you promised not to look!"

I looked still. "It must be devilish uncomfortable."

"No worse than your Blackspur's bellyband."

"But he has it removed each night, while you—"

"I do what I must, Conrad. Have I complained?"

"Heaven forfend." I tightly shut my eyes against the sight of the rest of her exposed sleekness. Like a song, her body was. Another moment and I might have less ease of conscience. "You've been an angel."

I dove for my clean braies and patched hose, my tattered motley and freshly polished boots.

Entering the great hall of the monastery with jingling bells and rattling marotte, I saw it with new eyes. With my hunger appeased and shivering banished, the benches full of tonsured friars sprang at me. They lounged in comfort across the tables, cups of wine in hand, casting long shadows from the light of torches ranged against the walls. Many torches. More torches than Otto used for even the highest of feast days. And between the torches were rich hangings worked in gold and silver, and roaring fires, and—

"A song!" proclaimed the figure dominating the head table. The abbot? He looked noble enough: the long, finely boned face showing perhaps forty years of living; arrow-sharp eyes; streaks of silver beginning to dominate the thick, dark hair surrounding his tonsured pate. "A song to warm our hearts, next a story to fill our heads till compline prayers and bed be rung!"

Tossing my marotte to Christa, I leaped into a set of cartwheels that took me jangling through the hall to the abbot himself. Made a deep bow. By Saint Paul, but my limbs were rusty.

"Gracious thanks for your hospitality, Lord Abbot—"

He brushed off the title with a wave of slim, elegant fingers. "Saint Francis had no patience for abbots. I am but the guardian of my brothers."

I bowed again.

"Guardian dear, what cheer? Love or death or battle? Pray tell us what to prattle!"

"*Love!*" roared the monks.

"*Love,*" sighed the guardian.

By the time pipe was in hand, Christa was at my side. We gave them love. We gave them "Unter den Linden." Three times we gave them "Unter den Linden," till Christa's sweet voice had half the monks sobbing in their cups. Whispering to her "This won't do," I piped into a round of jigs. As my capering feet stopped before the greatest of the fires, I swung back to my audience.

"Love is well to swell the heart . . . yet for a night so

cold—what better way to hold you smart than gird your minds with murder? The tale I tell may oft be told, but pray let me unfold . . . none other than the foulest death of the boldest of the bold!"

"Siegfried!" shouted a good brother.

"From *The Song of the Nibelungs*—" I tried adding, before being shouted down.

"Give us Siegfried!"

To the enthusiastic pounding of cups and stamping of sandals, I launched into the jealous treachery of the wicked knight Hagen and King Gunther in their plot to kill the greatest of German heroes. Soon I was lost within my own web of telling.

> *As there the noble Siegfried to drink o'er the*
> > *fountain bent,*
> *Through the cross he pierced him, that from the*
> > *wound was sent*
> *The blood nigh to bespatter the tunic Hagen*
> > *wore.*
> *By hand of knight such evil deed shall wrought*
> > *be nevermore.*

"Nevermore," came a soft, echoing sigh.

I searched through the shadows to find Christa sprawled near my feet, firelight dancing over her golden hair. "Aye," I murmured. "Play upon my verse."

And as I unfolded the tale, so she did, sending sighs and

groans, gasps and ghastly gurgles through the rapt hush of the great hall. In truth, that night did Siegfried take longer in dying than any mortal man before or since. And why not? Did not darkness and the weather magically enfold us? Did not the assembly value us? Thus, taking my cue from Christa, I cast aside the verse to *become* Siegfried.

"Cowards!" I spat at the closest shadows. "This is how I am repaid for all my faithful service?" I writhed in agony. "Curses upon you and yours—even unto eternity!"

A death rattle stopped me yet again. There was Christa shaking my marotte most dramatically. Trying to ignore the bauble, I moved forward to Siegfried's ruing of his lady wife, Kriemhild; to his last will and testament—

"Revenge!" Christa howled.

I gently booted her to silence for my concluding stanza.

All around the flowers were wetted with the
    blood
As there with death he struggled. Yet not for
    long he could,
Because the deadly weapon had cut him all too
    sore;
And soon the stout and noble knight was
    doomed to speak no more.

A keening cry swept through the hall as I sank to the floor. Jerked. Lay still. I glared at my sparrow, and she artfully tapered her wail to a most wistful, woeful moan. Had I created a monster? It was not the moment to dwell on the thought. Cheers filled the hall as I sprang back to life for my bow. I held out my hand for Christa to join me, and the cheers grew. Brother Sebastian waddled up to us with two cups and a flagon of wine as compline bells rang.

"Oh, most excellent! You will do very well, indeed, Conrad the Good and Christof the Fair!"

I had not the time even to blink at our renaming before we were rushed off to our separate cells for the night. Before disappearing into hers, Christa winked and raised her cup to me.

"Only consider to what effect a rattling sword and shield could be used in your next retelling of Siegfried!"

"By Saint Peter, Christ—"

Out came her tongue. "Sweet dreams, Conrad the Good!"

I slammed into my barren cell to the pitiful solace of its narrow cot. Glowered past the guttering flame of the tiny oil lamp set in a niche below a rough wall painting of Saint Francis himself. Calmed enough to notice my hands.

Ho.

Somewhere along the way I had mislaid my cup, but I still gripped the near-full flagon of wine. I tipped it to my lips and tasted of it—robust and not too sweet—yet but a poor substitute for my sparrow's warmth. Another sip. What was one last lonely night? Had I not already endured thousands of them? I settled flagon and myself upon the bed. Come the morrow, Christa and I would be on the road again and free.

NINE

Father William's third and final volume had been a most handsomely illuminated book of hours. It was filled with short devotions, but I'd never more than quickly scanned the prayers. Instead, I'd spent long, breathless moments admiring the tiny vines and flowers and creatures creeping around the margins. But always I would stop myself to return to the front of the book—and its illustrated calendar for each month of the year. This inkling of what weather the seasons might bring intrigued me. December's picture had shown a peasant crouched before his cottage fire, trapped by the elements. Heavy December snow I could understand, yet here was November hardly begun. . . .

Somehow I had blithely passed over the good friars' talk of entrapment for the winter. Snow might ensnare Otto within the walls of his castle. It might hold Saint Francis's Little Brothers from the open road. But what had a few feet of snow to do with me and mine and our noble quest? Blackspur had power enough to surge through such stuff once the tempest was past.

The stroke of prime jolted me awake—and sent the empty flagon tumbling to the floor.

Christ's wounds! The wine that succored by night turned tormentor with the dawn.

Rubbing my aching head, with many a groan I deserted my chill, windowless cell to stagger through mazelike corridors in search of the courtyard and morning. At last, a likely door . . . I heaved—

"By God's passion!"

There was no morning.

Through a charcoal sky, more snow fell. Seeing the path plowed by the oaken door through a thickness greater than three feet, I knew it had never stopped falling. Never would stop falling, and my heart with it.

Trapped.

A sudden blast from the very core of Hell itself near swept me from my feet. I grasped for the doorjamb and hauled myself inside, then struggled to shut the door.

"How ice and fire can both be birthed in the same infernal place—" I muttered.

"The last ring of the Ninth Circle of Hell," came a voice. "There you will find your answer."

I spun. Here was a friar.

He bobbed his head. "Brother Thomas, Keeper of the Library. Do you read?" he asked. "And do you read Latin?"

"Yes to both," I managed to answer while wrapping my arms around my motley and wishing I'd not given up the warm novice robe.

"Then join me now, and I will endeavor to offer answers to your question."

I glanced around. "The others. Do you not need to pray with them?"

He smiled and shook his head. "We are not a contemplative order, thus are not restricted by devotions. My brothers may pray or sleep, as they like. They are a goodly fraternity, but few thinkers—or readers—are among them." Brother Thomas grasped my arm. "Do you know the work of the poet Dante Alighieri? Do you know his *Divine Comedy?* He had the courage to write in the vernacular—in Italian— but as I have no Italian, I am most grateful for our Latin translation. I believe I shall start you on his *Inferno.* I do find it the most compelling part. . . ."

My head whirled at this turn of events. *My head.* Even that blast from Hell itself had not cleared the results of my foolishness. Next there was my discovery of the true facts of winter on the road. . . . Very gingerly I allowed myself to be led away.

"I've found you at last!"

The breathless proclamation made me twist from the lectern where I'd been head to head with Brother Thomas over a particularly tricky bit of Latin verse. Any sudden motion was a mistake.

"Conrad!" Christa cried. "Are you ill?"

I grasped the lectern shelf for balance. "Only with regret."

She considered my deplorable state as the librarian himself turned . . . spied Christa . . . attacked.

"Christof the Fair," he sighed. Then, "Do you read? Do you read Latin?"

"Nay, but Conrad means to teach me at first opportunity."

"Although Saint Francis prized action over literacy, I beg to differ on this subject. And there is no time like the present." Reaching for her arm, he continued, "I happen to have access to an especially fine ABC!"

Christa extracted herself with grace. Offered a winsome smile. "Many thanks, Brother . . ."

"Thomas." A blush spread from cowl-collar up his plump, pink cheeks. He blinked owlishly. "Brother Thomas."

"Many thanks, Brother Thomas. But the lessons will wait for another moment. Conrad and I have need to practice for our evening performance."

"We do?" I dumbly asked.

"We do."

Firmly taking me in hand, my sparrow rushed me from the library.

❋ ❋ ❋

"Pull yourself together, Conrad. We must talk."

She hauled me into a small chamber decorated only with chair and kneeler. A private confessional? Shut the door. Turned on me.

"Sit, in Heaven's name, before you collapse upon the floor!"

Shakily did I sink into the chair. My stomach had also turned traitor. It roiled in perfect tempo with my skull.

"Whatever ails you?"

I squinted at her, hands on her hips, perfectly composed. Too perfectly. *She'd* retired with but a half-filled cup. "Wine," I admitted.

"You *are* an innocent!" she exclaimed. "Had you no notion of the effects of too much wine?"

"How *was* I to know?" I moaned. "Personally? Never before did I possess an entire flagon of it!" I clutched my churning belly and completed my confession. "My cell was so cold . . . and lonely without you."

"Silly goose!" Christa absolved me with a hug. "What you need is the hair of the dog that bit you. Pray, do not move. I've discovered the kitchen and will go to beg it."

Move? Heaven forfend. Unless it be to lay my spinning head upon the flat, *unmoving* solidness of the slate floor. . . . Yet even that goal was beyond me. Instead, I nodded off to visions of Otto's hounds in full cry, with me their quarry. Fang and his fellows were making short work of my new boots—and me within them—when she returned, replacing the dream with a bowl. I concentrated on the contents to the further curdling of my stomach.

"Most villainous!" I yelped. "What *is* this evil concoction?"

"A little something Lord Otto favored. Drink!"

Otto again. Shudders racked my body. Yet Christa hovered over me still, like some avenging angel. What choice had I? I raised the bowl and drank deeply. Gagged—

"By Satan himself!"

My dove smirked. "The Prince of Darkness was present only in the temptation. Herein lies your penance: raw eggs and herbs, much pepper, and brandy—"

"Stop!"

As the bowl crashed to the floor, I searched wildly for a place to heave. Slapped a hand over my mouth—

Banished to the emptiness of my cell, I abandoned the entire benighted day for the cold comfort of the hard, narrow bed. Christa had the final word from the doorway through which she'd escorted me.

"Dear, dear Conrad . . . when you have made recovery from your folly, then may we speak of monasteries and snow and loneliness."

"Blackspur!"

I threw my arms around my friend's neck and hugged. Breathed in the pungent, comforting smell of him, as if it had been years since our parting rather than a single day. He shook me loose to nuzzle my face.

"What have I done, Blackspur? All I've achieved by escaping Otto the Dumb—now Otto the Wrathful—is landing my sparrow and me within the walls of a monastery for the duration of winter!"

That it was no passing nightmare had been proved to me most forcefully this morning. Waking clear of head at last—by God's grace and Satan's potion—I'd rolled out of my lambskin. *Where had that come from? And the waiting brown woolen habit?* No matter, I'd accepted both. After flowing through my exercises, I'd donned robe and cloak and made a second attempt at the courtyard. Shoved mightily at the door. . . .

Mercy.

True, the storm had abated at last. Yet it had graced us with another foot of snow. Or more. It looked to be all the snow in the world. All the snow in the universe. I'd whistled my dismay into the blue-black stillness. From clear across the courtyard came a faint answering neigh.

Blackspur.

I'd forgotten the better half of me. Had he been fed? Watered? Had he been given the touch of human kindness?

Whistling a reply, I'd raced inside to rampage till I found the necessary tool: a shovel.

The moon sank. The sky lightened. Prime bells rang— before my roofless tunnel had reached the stable door. . . .

"Blackspur," I murmured yet again through the dimness. I backed away from his welcome heat to stow the shovel, to brush matted snow from my garments—and stumbled over a lantern.

"Ho! Here am I playing the fool yet again, with help at hand." I fumbled beneath layers for my pouch and flint. . . .

"And there was light!"

I could swear my horse laughed. In happiness to see me again? Or at my idiotic emotions? Only then did I examine his water: his trough was freshly filled. Examined his fodder: goodly hay overflowed his manger. Examined his coat: groomed to a fault. His stall had been cleaned. Even his bridle shone with polish.

"So." I turned back to give him the eye. "You *do* laugh at me. Ingrate. While you've been lolling in the attentions of your mysterious patron, I've been worrying for you. Worrying for your loneliness without me—"

"*Hee-haw!*"

I spun. Peeking his head over the top of Blackspur's stall was a donkey—a donkey with ears so long, they made mockery of my poor artificial ones. This creature had I missed in the excitement of our arrival. As I watched, Blackspur spurned me to caress the ass's furry head. I leaned around the wooden partition. *Her* furry head. For once wordless, I could do naught but shrug.

"Your snow tunnel is quite masterful—"

I spun again.

"—but would it not have been easier to visit Blackspur through the passage from the monastery?"

"Christa." Sighing, I slumped against a bale of hay.

"Christof the Fair, if you please. And are you certain these monks have taken vows of chastity? By the Holy Virgin, I swear they must see through my disguise, for upon my approach, I witness naught but lovesickness on every face."

My next sigh came forth from the very depths of my soul. "It is going to be a long, long winter, sparrow."

TEN

Praised be the Lord
For our Brother the Wind
And for Air and Cloud,
Calms and all Weather.

Francis of Assisi is surely the greatest among
saints, and the most patient. Within his benedic-
tion come creatures great and small . . . and all
of Nature. Living within Nature's whims, I—like
Brother Thomas—am tempted to take exception.

As flurries followed upon storms in a relentless pattern, the shovel became my constant companion.
The Little Brothers smiled as they watched me
trudge to the courtyard each morning. Just another folly of
their winter fool—though perhaps not quite as futile as my
quest for an "enlightened" lord. Not one chose to join me as

I slowly and carefully expanded my original tunnel path to the stable. The walls of snow grew to enormous heights, blocking the open-sided cloister walk lining the courtyard where the friars might take the air, come more clement weather.

Besides expanding my muscles, such labor brought me visions of the road beyond the monastery's shelter. In my mind's eye, this highway was irrevocably being covered to ever greater depths and heights—till snow must reach the very treetops. Yet I forbore clearing a path to the entry gate. Forbore any attempt to pry open that gate for a view of the world beyond. Better to keep my dismay within limits.

At last, I reached my present goal: creating a space large enough to exercise—or at least walk—Blackspur in the open air. Flinging down the shovel, I joyfully cartwheeled to my waiting friend. There I found his oft-invisible patron— Brother Josef, Keeper of the Stable. Nodding a greeting, I reached for my horse's halter.

"What madness do you now attempt, Conrad?"

"Blackspur needs to feel the elements, see the sky, else lose his strength ere spring return."

"Nonsense." The friar continued to placidly stuff the mangers with sweet-smelling hay. "Even our cows and sheep and goats are kept within covered shelters these long months."

"Aye, and I would not be the friar assigned to walk within such bottled air!"

Usually unflappable, he curled his lips within his gray

73

beard. "Such is the work given our novices . . . that they be made mindful of their brother creatures."

"And how many of this number choose to take their final vows with the spring?"

I received no answer, but little matter. Blackspur was dancing with impatience as I slipped the halter over his head. "So, my friend, *you* are ready to see Brother Sun."

I began walking him toward the door—

"Hee-haw, hee-haw, hee-haw, hee-haw!"

Blackspur dug in his hooves and arched his neck, yanking the lead rope from out my hands.

"By all the blessed saints in Paradise!"

Only the horse of a fool would fall in love with an ass. Martha—so named, Brother Josef had assured me, in honor of the sister of Mary and Lazarus, "because she is destined to do all the work"—did *not* wish to be left behind. I turned to Josef. "Does Martha need a halter?"

He shrugged acceptance of this latest folly. "In such a small space? She will be content to follow."

Thus I led the beasts forth to my gift of Brother Sun's rare smile.

Christa, knowing my feelings for Blackspur, had offered her assistance in my snow-clearing plan.

"Your time would be better spent in the library, sparrow. Learning your letters."

"But Brother Thomas—"

"Is quite harmless. Only look upon him! His imagination is tempered by his cowardice."

And it was so.

❋ ❋ ❋

Meanwhile, I spent my free hours in the library as well—making a rough translation of Dante's *Inferno* into my vernacular of German.

Abandon all hope, ye who enter here.

Such were the words cut in stone above the very gateway into Hell. Like some witch's curse these words were, sucking the gathered lost souls with the force of despair into the very arms of Charon. The narrative that followed was more than an allegory. This Dante had created the greatest dramatic story I had ever encountered—and I meant to add it to my repertoire. Would not my father be pleased by the endeavor?

Thus matters stood as November froze into December. Advent was upon us. The great Feast of Christmas approached. Christa and I planned a special play to glorify the Lord Jesus's birth—for which Blackspur and Martha and a few sheep would be honored with roles.

Truth be told, the two of us had few free moments alone to bemoan either the monastery, the snow, or loneliness. We paid for our shelter and hot baths and suppers each night with entertainment that brought us our only closeness. We learned to work in such tandem that I wondered

75

what had possessed me to scorn my sparrow's clever offerings that Great Tempest Night, which had brought us into the Franciscans' welcoming arms. More, we learned by force of necessity to live within Saint Francis's rule of celibacy. While our chasteness surely was admirable in the eyes of Heaven, I could not but think on Dante's star-crossed lovers in the Second Circle of Hell. I began feeling like a Paolo to Christa's Francesca, damned forever to be swept apart by infernal winds—seeing, yet never touching, my beloved. Thus our longing increased till I feared for the moment when one of us broke under the strain.

Yet slowly I was mastering the rhythms and wry humor of these Little Brothers. Slowly I began to accept as a gift this reprieve winter had given us.

Brother John was ensconced on a stool in the center of our first night's changing room—now our practice room— trying once more to balance my three juggling balls in the air. As always, he frowned ferociously with the effort, emphasizing the rough angles of his bony nose, which matched his oversize Adam's apple. Since he had but a few years more than I, dexterity should have been his—yet the gangly friar was all disjointed wrists and elbows. I snatched the balls from their fatal plunge and set them spinning, higher and higher.

"You must think of them as rising to Heaven, John, not descending to Hell!"

"That I could have but this one gift of yours, Conrad."

He studied his equally bony fingers, then cracked his knuckles forlornly. "Then when I go forth for my first preaching in the spring, how easy it would be to demonstrate the mystery of the Holy Trinity!"

I took compassion on him. "Pray to the Lord Jesus. It is his night of nights, is it not? And relax your arms. Your entire body. You try too hard!"

Nonchalantly keeping the balls reaching for the firmament, I glanced around the chaos of the chamber where Christa and I worked on our entertainments. It was a pity Brother John had adopted *us* and *it* nearly from the moment of our arrival—thus dashing any hopes the room might be a private haven for my songbird and me. Yet there was no future in brooding over chances lost. The stage-befuddled young friar had not been without his uses. My eyes lit on the latest example.

"By Saint Paul! Well done, Brother!" He smiled as I caught the falling orbs and dropped them into his hands. "You've purloined the goods!"

Draped over the odds and ends we'd amassed were the very robes of the chapel's Virgin Mary: the richest silk of the deepest blue the Orient could produce, lovingly bordered with embroidery of gold.

"Aye, and I'd best be preparing myself in them," Christa pointedly announced.

Our thick-skulled helper ignored all implications, hopefully tossing the balls yet again.

"John," I ordered, "it is time to see to the animals."

"Never fear, Conrad"—he lunged for a ball and missed—"Brother Josef and Brother Anselm have them well in hand."

I seized the balls and stuffed them into the pouch of his cowl. "Go practice in the great hall. The height of the arches will grant you closer proximity to the Almighty. And while you are doing so, make certain our stage has not been tampered with."

"No one would touch it, Conrad!"

"*John.*" I yanked him to his feet. "Christof must change for our Christmas Eve festivities. And he is *still* shy."

"Oh." Brother John blinked recognition at last. Mumbling "A thousand pardons," he scurried off in embarrassed imitation of that first night.

I swung toward Christa, sudden doubts assailing me like gathering storm clouds.

"Are you certain this is a good idea, sparrow?"

"Of course I am not certain"—she shrugged off her robe—"but when I begin to doubt my own sex . . . It is this, or go mad!"

Now there was a soft shirt beneath the robes. Even braies. I grinned. Then she was turning away. Slipping from the braies. Slipping from the shirt. Loosing her breast band—

"What are you doing?" I near barked, but it came out a moan.

"The Virgin Mary was a woman, Conrad. Like me."

"But—"

"The brothers will think it only another improvement of the stage. For this role, I will walk free."

I yanked at my lengthening hair. "You would play with fire. Tempt the Fates—"

"Nay. I would feel like—*be*—a woman for one brief hour. Consolation enough to survive the coming months."

The band fell, melting all my protests. Christa shook her golden head and turned toward me, tall and proud.

"You have no reason to doubt your sex," I whispered. "None at all." If this be the result of too much strain, I could live with the consequences. I caught her within the coarse wool of my habit. Brushed a newly roughened cheek against hers.

She nuzzled it contentedly. "I have been longing to feel your beard, Conrad."

"I did not think you'd taken notice—"

"I take note of everything about you. The way you lean into the lectern, as if you would devour your precious Dante, the way—"

Kissing her neck stilled her tongue—for a brief moment.

"The beard will be red . . . like your hair."

"In the fullness of time." In the here and now, I luxuriated in the softness of her skin, the rightness of her curves, then made to pull back. "This might not be the best moment—"

"Christmas Eve? It is a time of miracles, is it not?"

Her arms tightened around me, till I could do naught

but enfold her once more in my own. "What miracle do you seek, sparrow?" I murmured.

"Above all . . . to be betrothed this night of nights."

"The most simple of miracles," I breathed. "I take you, Christa the Fair, for my betrothed."

"And I you, Conrad the Good," she whispered. "I have always taken you for my betrothed. Though it mean the coldest bed of snow—"

"—or contending with the very Hounds of Hell for our supper."

"Or"—we smiled with the same thought—"yet another monastery winter!"

As our lips met, sealing the contract—

Blows rained upon the door.

"The friars await you! The animals await you!"

"Brother John," Christa groaned.

"Give us but another moment!" I begged, thrusting my beloved toward her silks. "We come anon!"

Blackspur capered down the center aisle of the crowded great hall. I rode in motley upon his back, waving a festive flag and crying the play's banns as if gathering an audience for a town performance:

> Glorious God, Lord most of might,
> Who made Heaven and Earth, both sea and
> land—
> And the angels above, to serve Him bright.

Mankind, too, He made with His hand,
And our lovely Lady, that lantern of light,
To give us Lord Jesus, our Earth's great delight!
The babe Jesus would we sing, till all are made
merry—
Christ save you all who would listen and tarry!

Vaulting from Blackspur, I bowed before Gregory the Guardian for benediction.

"Well spoken, Conrad the Good. You, too, have been a gift from Heaven." He blessed me with the sign of the cross and a rare smile. "You may proceed."

Another bow and I was walking my horse to the stable-stage we'd built at the head of the hall. "Stay, Blackspur," I directed him. "Your best part is yet to come."

Disappearing behind the flimsy walls, I tugged off my cap and shrugged into my robe. Reaching into the pail of fresh snow I'd ordered, I liberally daubed myself in its coldness. Next I reached through a gap in the wall for fistfuls of manger hay to scatter about my person for a touch of bona fides. With the addition of a waiting staff, my costume was complete. Hunching my shoulders, I lamely hobbled to the front of our set as Brother Anselm shoved three confused sheep toward me from the right-hand corridor. They bleated most piteously, giving me my cue.

"Lord, but these weathers be cold!" I moaned. "E'en my sheep protest neath their wool—and me ne'er so well dressed as they! Aye and forsooth, we poor shepherds have the worst of life's lot . . . crippled, chapped, robbed of our rest!" I paused, for here was Brother John's entrance—

"Bless us and Dominus!" he bellowed as he emerged from the left—and promptly froze before the overflowing hall.

Lord save us. The fright had taken him. Would he remember the rest? "The wind . . . ," I hinted.

John shuddered as if in its throes, then bravely soldiered on. "Aye, the wind is full keen, the frosts so hideous. . . . Yet we who walk such nights oft see sudden sights when other men do sleep."

" 'Tis true enow." I hobbled closer to offer a comradely pat on the arm. It gave him such encouragement that he pulled away to dramatically thrust his staff toward the arched ceiling. Indeed, he thrust with such enthusiasm that the juggling balls still within the pouch of his hood near shook loose. I concentrated on them as if they were the very Star of Bethlehem itself. They *would not* spill, tripping the sheep. . . .

"Take yon star, Mak." John gulped, swallowing the last of his fears through his bobbing Adam's apple. With relish, he strode a few bold, unrehearsed steps forward. "It shines much too bright." He leaned back to squint, and back yet more . . . emptying his hood. "By the Holy Rood—means it evil or good?"

I stumbled past a wandering sheep to kneel beneath John's upraised arm, groping furiously for the balls. One . . . Where were the second and third? "Nay, I cannot say. . . ." Shifted my line of sight. "But who comes this way?"

Enter from the rear: Christa astride Martha, with Brother Thomas obligingly trudging by her side as the torch-bearing Joseph. As they neared the first tables, the friars began leaning toward the halo of light encircling Christa, the halo of light emphasizing her freed breasts. How proudly they rose beneath the shimmering silk. There was that about her . . . a girl-woman innocence, an on-the-brink purity. . . . As my heart pounded within me, a low hum rose. Intensified. Martha slowly bore her burden farther still into the great hall—

Chaos broke forth.

"A *miracle!*"

"The Virgin herself comes!"

"Appearing among us!"

John and I abandoned all pretense of playacting to stare as raptly as the others at the unfolding scene. I had heard tales of religious frenzies and ecstatic experiences . . . but my Christa as the cause? For here was she, of a sudden surrounded by prostrate, wailing friars.

"*Holy Mary, Mother of God.*" The prayer rose like incense to fill the arches of the ceiling, spreading to saturate every hidden space of the great hall.

"*Pray for us sinners!*"

Withal, Christa managed to retain her queenly poise, and her seat. It was a miracle in itself. But it could not last. For Blackspur *did not* stay for his scene by the manger. Before my disbelieving eyes, he trotted back down the center aisle, scattering the kneeling, bobbing, and swaying monks; trotted back to his donkey-love.

"*Nay*," I breathed.

What use? The threads of our monastery life were unraveling before my eyes. My horse only widened the gap as he proudly executed the new trick I'd been at pains to school him in. Magnificently did he sit back on his haunches. Elegantly did he tuck his forelegs under him. Adoringly did he bow his head in honor of the waiting Martha—and the Virgin.

"*Even the creatures pay tribute!*"

A great roar filled the hall.

"*Praise the Lord God! A true miracle!*"

Blackspur's obeisance was the last straw. I watched my sparrow's face turn white. Watched her begin to waver in her seat—

"*Christa!*"

Belaboring all before me with my staff, I rushed to her rescue—and promptly tripped flat on the two lost juggling balls. Whereupon the newly emboldened sheep made haste to hedge me in. As one, they lunged for my artistically arranged sprigs of hay—

Mercy.

Our deception revealed, I flung my arms over my head in utter defeat.

ELEVEN

*Have mercy on Me, God, have mercy on Me—
since in Thee does My soul trust. And in the
shadow of Thy wings shall I hope—until iniquity
passes over.*

*Thus wrote Saint Francis in his third psalm. And
thus I prayed in the many days to come.*

"This won't do."

Gregory the Guardian gazed upon Christa and me as we stood at attention before the parchment-littered desk where he sat in judgment. A sad gaze, I thought.

"It won't do at all."

I racked my brain for a clever response. In rhyme. My mind was as frozen as my legs. This was no Otto to be idly tweaked with foolery. The Little Brothers had opened their arms to us. They had treated us fairly, treated us like human beings—not like unbaptized dregs of humanity. I hung my head. Yet beside me, Christa did not.

"What would you have of us, good Father?"

I raised my head to catch the flash of defiance I knew would be in my kestrel's eyes.

"We entertained you fairly. We lived honorably by your rules. We tried to bring the true spirit of Christmas to you—"

"And succeeded. Only too well." The guardian smiled wryly despite himself. "Half my brothers still believe you to be the Virgin Mary incarnate, Christof—" He shrugged. "Excuse me . . . Christa. Half my brothers will never be dissuaded from that belief. The other half stand in thrall to your very gender." He spread his arms. "This is my given work: to guard the moral and physical well-being of my simpler brothers." A pause. "At least during their winter sojourn. If some few fall to the temptation of a woman's embrace during their time in the world . . ." A wearier shrug. "But not on my watch. Can you understand my dilemma?"

Christa nodded acceptance.

"Thus . . ." He hesitated, as if his decision were as painful to him as it surely would be to us. "Thus I must ask you both to leave our consecrated grounds."

Cast out into the cold.

What other solution could there be?

"Yet . . ." Another pause, then he directed himself to Christa. "Yet I think it best to hold to your disguise. Outside the protection of our walls, you will find that the greater world does not make such fine distinctions . . . or give such gentle remonstrations as we here do." He stood and came before us. "Still, I would send you forth with my blessing, and the blessing of Saint Francis—for was he not called 'God's jester'? You have won a place in the hearts of all the Little Brothers, and we, too, will suffer from your absence." He raised an arm over us in benediction—

"Wait!" I pleaded. "A boon I would ask!"

The arm dropped. "Speak."

"Please"—I reached for Christa's hand—"marry us before God ere we leave this holy place."

Her fingers gripped mine in hope, then loosed as the guardian shook his head sorrowfully. "You know it is forbidden me to give a holy sacrament to the unbaptized."

I fell to my knees. "I alone am unbaptized. I pray to the Lord God Almighty that you would release my soul from this injustice!"

"Good Conrad." He sighed. "You would try my patience. You are clever. You know full well the edicts of Holy Mother Church regarding your kind—edicts that have stood since the Church Fathers declared all forms of theater the very armory and forge of Satan's weapons!"

Yet these many weeks have you and your brothers enjoyed the fruits of my "infernal" armory.

This thought I did not voice. Instead, my head began aching with a new riddle: Without baptism, I could not be married. No chicken came without the egg. How, then, to attain the egg? I stared straight up into Gregory's eyes. "Tell me. How am I to be saved?"

Running a hand through his thick, silvery hair, the guardian began pacing his small chamber. "There is baptism by water, of which you are well aware." Another circuit before us. "Then there is baptism by the shedding of blood, a gift given to blessed martyrs. Finally"—he stopped and planted himself firmly before me—"there is baptism by the fire of faith." His ascetic face shone with the firmness of belief. "The just man shall be saved."

And in the interim, my beloved and I must live on platitudes. Would that the gentle and wise Francis had been standing in Gregory's sandals.

I rose from my knees. "Your blessing, then, and away we'll be bound, the sooner the good master of my quest be found."

Brother Josef watched with Christa in silence as I prepared Blackspur. With all in readiness, he handed me a sack.

"Oats for yon beast. God go with ye."

"Many thanks."

I packed the offering, took my horse in hand—

And Martha let loose a bray that near sundered my heart . . . and Blackspur's, too. His head darted between the two of us, eyes wild, heart pumping fit to burst his mighty chest.

"Blackspur, Blackspur." I captured his neck to murmur

in his ear. "Life is not fair. It is not kind. . . . True love must oft be left behind. Poor substitute that I be, I am your friend." I rubbed his nose, caught his eye. "And I have need of you. My sparrow, too."

Blackspur pulled from my grasp, wrung a soulful neigh from the very depths of his being—and followed.

Outside, Christmas morn was crisp and still. I looked with wonder on what had been wrought in the holiness of the night: Many hands had plowed a path to the gate. Many hands had freed that gate till it opened to the world. Beyond, the same hands had cleared a path to the waiting road. All for us. Shaking my head, I set Christa behind the saddle. Made ready to join her—

"Stay!"

Here came Brother Thomas and, behind him, Brother John. I waited while Thomas fumbled a parcel into my hands.

"You'll be needing your translation of the *Inferno*." He squinted his owl eyes in the snow glare. "The first in *our* vernacular. Would that I'd had the time to copy it, for I believe it to be a fair rendition, catching the poetic niceties—"

John cleared his throat.

"Yes, yes." Thomas stretched another parcel up to Christa. "That your most excellent reading progress be not slowed by this untimely, most unfortunate departure."

My dove leaned down to place a kiss upon the brother's brow. "I shall miss you, Thomas."

As he backed off in confusion, John came to the fore,

carrying a set of leathern saddlebags. His Adam's apple bobbed. "The brothers having experience say, do you keep making toward the south. The mighty lords are more merciful there." He thrust the bags at me. Managed a smile. "I purloined your robes. The way is long and cold, and mayhap their warmth will comfort you."

Now I must sling the bags over my seat and truly set myself astride Blackspur, else the wetness of my eyes betray me. I grasped the reins—

"Nay, but watch!" John called.

I turned to see him pull my juggling balls from his open cowl. Watched as he sent them toward Heaven . . . and kept them spinning there.

"The truest of miracles!" I cried. "And my gift to you."

Swiping a sleeve across my face, I nudged Blackspur through the open gate.

Not south to mercy, but west to the unknown did our road now wander. Despite my worst imaginings, its snow did not reach to the treetops. The bowing firs lining the way had served as a tunnel through which the wind had swept its surface near clear. Yet as Blackspur crunched his hooves through the highway's pristine, icy skin, no songs accompanied him. Neither my songbird nor I could find the heart for it. The rest of that Christmas Day progressed in silence. Christa's arms around my waist, her head upon my shoulder, were sorrowing comfort till the sun began descending behind its haze. Blackspur plodded on, deep in his own mourning, till I could no longer ignore the coming night.

"We must find shelter," I murmured.

Christa stirred behind me. "We passed one deserted village. Could there be another ahead?"

I shivered, but not because of the rising wind. "I would not stop in one. The spirits—"

"*Ghosts?* I cannot conceive you believe in them, Conrad!"

"You did not spend your baby years wandering through plague-ravaged lands." I fought down the prickle in my spine, the eerie remembrance of *loss* filling the very air in such places. "The forest preserved us our first night. We will throw ourselves on its mercy yet again." So saying, I spied what I'd been seeking: the glistening path of a frozen stream leading into the woodland's hidden heart.

"Ho, Blackspur!"

I set my mount onto its slick course.

Our cold haven did not welcome us as that first night glade had. Searching through sodden fallen branches for something that might burn into warmth, I could think only of Dante's infernal Dark Forest. Would these knotted tree limbs bleed? Would they burst into the agonized voices of imprisoned sinners as they had in the Seventh Circle of Hell? In the end, half expecting Harpies at my shoulder, I had need to steal from Blackspur's oats for tinder. Anything to banish some of the darkness as quickly as possible.

As the first flames flickered and grew, my misgivings began lifting with the rising smoke. Only then could I bask in Christa's smile as we stood over the struggling fire, warming our hands and trying to ignore the emptiness of our stomachs. "Your smile warms me better than the fire," I whispered.

She offered another, and with it a kiss, too. "How good it is to be able to make that gesture openly, Conrad! Could it be the brothers have given us a boon in turning us out of their sanctuary?"

I reached for her. "So long as we don't freeze to death in its freedom!"

"Verily." She pulled away. "Your arms are warm, yet John's gift of robes might make them warmer."

"Our lambskin, too."

I fetched our blanket to spread by the fire; next opened one of the saddlebags. Reached for a woolen habit. Felt something tucked within it—

"Christa! Dove!"

"What is it, Conrad?"

I ripped through both bags, presenting my finds. "Good bread! Rounds of cheese! A great length of smoked sausage! Even dried apples! Enough to see us through to the nearest town!"

Christa swept down like a hawk . . . attacked the same bags . . . whooped in triumph. "And wine! A whole flagon of it!"

"Nay." I waved away the temptation. "My taste for it be forever lost."

"Silly Conrad. There's no harm in moderation. It will warm us. But we must ration it like the food." So saying, she pulled the cork and sipped. I watched the shudder working down her frame.

"Even better." She grinned. "Brandy! And the finest."

"Are you certain? You'd best let me try. . . ."

Shortly our haunted forest was taking on a much friendlier glow. We layered the woolen robes over our garments, supped upon our favorite meal of toasted bread and cheese, and retired within our old lambskin cocoon.

"Sparrow," I murmured to her head atop my lap, "think you we may begin again where we left off before the monastery?"

She considered my question for long moments. "In part," she answered at last. "But there have been unexpected changes. Now I can read better than Lady Ermengud ever could. . . ." She nestled closer. "And I can better help you with your work . . . and we are betrothed. . . ."

A new emptiness hit me with a pang. "But not married."

"Stop fretting, Conrad. The Lord Jesus Himself and all the holy saints know our intentions are honorable and pure. If we would be married, we must take it upon ourselves . . . for surely the Church and the world will not give *this* boon to us."

"As easily as that?" I wondered.

"A surety," she said with conviction. "But we must make our own ceremony—to celebrate the sacredness of our vows."

"When?"

She snuggled more closely still. "As you wisely told me at the start of our adventure . . . when the moment is ripe. But not this night. . . . I truly have neither the strength nor the proper disposition . . . with the sorrow of leaving our friends—"

"And the brandy?"

Her lips curled sweetly. "And the brandy. Both have drained me."

"Sleep, then." As I bent to kiss her cheek, a wild howl filled the blackness of the forest. Christa near leaped from her skin to cling to me.

"*Spirits?*"

Other howls followed. Closer. Much closer.

Dante's Hounds of Hell. Come to finish the Harpies' work.

The fire collapsed into embers. Nothingness closed in.

The howls returned. Yet these voices had depth and variety—becoming almost a conversation.

"Not spirits. *Wolves.*"

Tearing myself away, I reached for my knife. "Hide yourself within the blanket. For the love of God, do not move. Do not cry out."

I bounded up, first to the saddlebags, next to bring Blackspur closer. He was awake and trembling. I caught his neck. "You must not speak either, my friend. Be strong with me."

Tying him near Christa, I threw more knotty wood upon the fire, expecting cries of *"Men we were. . . . Is there no pity left in any soul?"*

When only the crackle of consuming flames returned to me, I forced Dante from my head. His verse could not teach me to survive this new ring of Hell . . . yet mayhap the wisdom of another man could.

Setting my back to the reborn flames, I waited with weapons in hand: the flashing knife blade in one, and in the other—

They came.

Hollow panting surrounded our snowy glade . . . and yellow eyes. Even Dante could not imagine the terror I then felt. I tried to breathe in rhythm with their pants. Tried to feel the ravenous hunger of these beasts. Their *need*.

It was then Saint Francis placed his hand on me. Strength and utter calmness followed.

I took one step away from the fire, toward the brightest of those eyes.

"Brother Wolf. Come to me. In the name of Lord Jesus, come, and do no harm to any here."

The eyes blinked. As time itself stopped, the creature slunk forward, tail between his legs. In the flickering light, I could see how hard a winter it had been outside the monastery walls. Ribs protruded beneath his matted fur, bloody scars slashed his muzzle. His pant became a whimper.

"Brother Wolf," I whispered, "you have suffered more than I. Would there were enough for all your kin—but this only can I give."

I tossed him my other weapon—our precious sausage.

"Accept my gift and let there be peace between us."

With a snap of his jaws, he caught the long rope of meat. Barely breathing, I watched him wriggle from the clearing, sausage trailing behind. Listened as his brothers lunged for their share. Then I crouched by the fire to keep watch over my loved ones through the cold of the endless night.

TWELVE

*In every church are pictures of saints: Sebastian,
martyr of the blood, pierced with dripping arrows;
Ursula and her eleven thousand virgins, ravished
and slain by the Hun; Valentine, beaten by clubs
and beheaded; Stephen, stoned to a pulp; Vincent,
flesh gashed with iron hooks, then bound upon a
gridiron and roasted. . . . On every altar is
Christ crucified with thorns, nails, spears, and
more blood.*

*If Holy Mother Church be drenched in blood,
drenched in violence, only a fool would seek pity
from the world that Church encompasses. Verily,
without the compassion of Lord Jesus before his
death, without the mystery that was Francis of
Assisi—I could not save my soul from despair.*

I knew we were nearing a true town when I saw the gallows tree. Too well did I remember such trees from the wandering days with my father. They gave me nightmares still. Now I stared upon new nightmares to come. Silhouetted against a bloody sunset, five bodies swayed in the wind—four of them with the look of having given feast to buzzards through the early winter famine. Could even Saint Francis call these vilest of carrion eaters "brother"?

"Conrad!" Christa gasped. "What— Oh, *Conrad!*"

She buried her head in my back as I slowed Blackspur. There was something about the fifth. . . .

"Stop, Blackspur!" I ordered.

Gripping me painfully, Christa looked again. "The smallest one," she breathed in my ear. "He lives! By all that is holy, he lives!"

My horse smelled death. Nostrils quivering, he shied when I prodded him toward the tree. I bent over his neck. "It must come to us all," I whispered, "yet your time is not near. Courage!"

Blackspur rallied. Remembering his war charger's schooling, he shook his mane in the rising blast and leaped toward the bodies. Unerringly, the final kick of his hind legs halted us beneath the quick one. Without pause, without thought, did I raise my knife. *Slashed.* Harder and harder, with a growing rage did I hack through the thick hempen rope hoisting the body. One slash for the plague that left no pity upon the land . . . another for my benighted role in life . . . a third for our banishment from safe harbor. More would come, but with a hoarse wheeze, the last victim slumped full across Blackspur's neck—whereupon my much-tried friend bolted.

Not down the road into town but across the nearest snowy field he flew. I frantically clutched the body, while Christa just as frantically clutched at me. In the desperate attempt to keep our seats, it took a long moment to realize when Blackspur actually stopped. I looked up. Here was some peasant's outbuilding. I breathed again.

"By God's grace, shelter. With night falling fast, and with our new baggage—"

"I pray this be safer than the town!" Christa gasped. "Though whatever possessed you . . ."

My Furies had vanished with our mad flight. "All in wolfskin be not wolves" was my answer. "The present problem is how to unload ourselves."

Yet unload ourselves we did and soon were within the questionable shelter of the rough-hewn structure. I flung back my hood, then pulled my fool's cap tighter over my ears, setting its bells to jangling as I made a quick survey. The last of day's light creeping through unchinked gaps between timbers helped. The howling wind also creeping through those gaps did not. A shiver overtook me as I squinted harder. This place once held winter's stock of hay, yet it had been emptied of all but scraps only two months into the season. It did not take the logic of an Aquinas to put two and two together. Beyond lay a hungry, *angry* town. I turned to Christa.

"Scrape some hay together for Blackspur, please. If there be any left, gather more for our new acquaintance to lie upon." I searched for my flint and iron, then leaped to yank at a drooping rafter beam. Rotted through, part of it fell. I smiled. "This will answer for a fire."

"Will you pull down the very roof over our heads, Conrad?" Christa chided. "And what of its owner?"

"His lord has need to make improvements upon his fiefdom. I do but bring the fact to his attention." So saying, I proceeded to build our fire. When its light and heat were enough to give us modest succor, yet not enough to call down wrath from the distant huts—I was not that much of a fool—I yanked off my cap and turned to our hanged man. Lying on Christa's bed of hay, he seemed younger, so much younger than when swinging on that tree. . . . Truth struck me like a blow. "He's but a stripling who's yet to see ten years!"

"And near frozen to death." Christa shoved me aside, dragging our lambskin in one hand, clutching our flagon of brandy in the other.

"But—" I protested.

"Mercy is not a halfway thing, Conrad. You cut him down. Now are we accountable for the results." Efficiently did she wrap our warm blanket around the miscreant's pinched body. Gently did she lift his head and force some brandy between his lips. I knelt beside the two to watch his throat begin to work. Another sip—

"Landed in Heaven, have I?" Merry brown eyes opened upon the croak. "God's truth! Got me own ministering angel!"

Upon which, my sparrow smiled brighter than any Seraphim. "He'll live!"

"*Awww.*" But the lad's disappointment was brief. "Get to have another go at the whole mess, then, I wager." He fumbled open the clasp of his threadbare cloak. "Have a gander," he rasped. "My old man was a blacksmith. . . ." A pause to stare soulfully up at Christa. "Got any more of that tonic, Angel? By Christ's foe, it be strong enough to raise Lazarus all over again."

Christa tipped the bottle most profligately down the young scoundrel's throat. After which, he trembled violently . . . then miraculously found the strength to rise on an elbow. "Like I was saying." He shook his mop of black hair and grabbed at his neck. "Look here."

I bent with Christa.

"What in the world—"

"My old man, he always said I was born to be hanged. This here was his parting gift to me."

Around his scrawny neck was—

"A band of iron!" Christa exclaimed.

"Worked, too!" The boy beamed. " 'Course it weren't no treat left dangling the livelong, almighty freezing afternoon . . . kicking off them Hell-buzzards. . . . Without you coming along about then . . ." He sank back down, eyes closing, the ordeal beginning to take its toll.

"Wait!" I reached for his shoulder. Near shook it till I caught myself. "What did you *do?*"

"Snatched me a mutton haunch from the innkeeper's kitchen . . . on account of I was that famished. . . . Shame of it was, I never did get to eat it. . . ." His lids crept shut again.

"Please," Christa begged, "tell us your name."

We had to lower our heads for his answer.

"Max," he sighed. "Second Chance Max."

Was the Good Samaritan asked to freeze to death for his charity? Nay. On this principle, my dove and I also spent the night beneath the lambskin, spooned to either side of our young rogue. His teeth ground and chattered most fiercely, and the fever in him came and went, yet he slept withal. I did not. As the light of dawn forced its way through the timber's gaps surrounding us, I gave up the effort. Yet I was loath to leave the warmth, so I lay there considering Max of the Second Chance. Whatever would we do with him? It was plain we could not abandon him in *this* town. And now, neither could we use the town to replenish our dwindling food supplies. I had not the stomach even to enter such a place—

"Ey—" Max squirmed awake next to me and rubbed his eyes. Grinned. "Best night's sleep I can remember. Next for sommat in me belly—"

"—and you'll be a new man," Christa chuckled from his other side.

I stared across Max at my beloved. Sleep became her. She looked tousled and soft and inviting . . . and there was not a thing to be done about it. *Mercy.* My impetuous rescue had put yet another crimp in our courtship. With a growl, I rolled out from under the blanket and stomped across the dirt floor to Blackspur.

"What's amiss with my savior, then?" Max asked.

This time Christa laughed. "Morning does not always agree with Conrad the Good. Let him but see to his horse and do his exercises—"

"Exercises?"

"A proper jester must always begin the day with his exercises."

"Faith! I've fallen in with traveling players!"

The awe in young Max's voice made even me smile and turn from Blackspur's grooming. The boy was staring raptly at Christa again.

"And who be you?"

"Christof the Fair!" I bawled across the rafters in answer. Best get our roles properly sorted from the beginning. But Max only peered from Christa to me, then back again.

"Never be pulling my leg. If she's a he, then I'm a eunuch, and I be fair certain"—he tossed off the blanket and grabbed for his groin—"them good Christian burghers left me with me balls." A beatific smile crossed his face as he verified the truth of the fact. But by this point, Christa was doubled over, choking with mirth.

"By Saints Peter and Paul both!" I stomped back to them. "Here now, Christof—"

She reached for me. "I cannot play that game again, Conrad. Not yet. Even though he journey with us but a day."

"A day? On me own again in a day?" Max popped up in a sudden lather. "I don't give a bean what she calls herself. God's heart! She can call herself the Virgin Mary and I'll fall on me knees right proper—"

"Nay!" we both cried.

The looks on our faces stopped him but a moment before he plowed forward. "And I can be a help! That I can! Why I can foot a jig like nobody's business, and as for the morris dance—"

He was on those feet now, stamping out frantic steps. It was too much effort, too soon. His legs began crumpling beneath him. I leaped to catch his fall, yet even safely in my arms, he kicked still.

"*Please,*" he begged, "do but buy me a drum. I'll drum up far bigger crowds than ever you've seen. I'll *steal* a drum to play for you—"

"No more of this torture!" Christa pleaded. "He is breaking the very heart within me." She snatched the boy from out my grasp and laid him gently upon the lambskin.

"Max shall have his second chance. We will see how well he travels with us. We will see how he takes to our life. There is time to decide." She bobbed her head in decision. "And now I think we will eat."

The lad's face turned to adoration as he gazed up at Christa. "Thank you, Angel," he whispered.

My dove sighed. "The first rule: You must not call me 'Angel.' " The second rule: In the world, I am known as Christof and a *man*. Only in privacy am I Christa—a *woman*. A woman sacredly betrothed to Conrad."

"Anything you say, Angel."

"Thirdly," she continued, "we are not mere players but on a holy quest to find a good master." Christa caught my eye. "Have I forgotten anything, Conrad?"

"Only to seek my counsel in these weighty matters." I cleared my throat. What was done was done. "As to food, we have but cheese and dried apples remaining. I'm thinking it would not go amiss to buy a pot at the next town. And a little meat. A hot broth would be welcome for the coming night's cold."

Knowing me too well, Christa was not gulled by my sudden change of subject. She apologized with a brilliant smile. "Your scars have taught me compassion, dearest Conrad. I've but played the fool's part for you."

I shrugged forgiveness, and she laid a hand on young Max's brow. I could tell from her frown that his fever had returned. "We'll buy herbs, too. It's time I collected a medicine kit for our journey." She tucked the lambskin around the boy, then rose to be gathered in my arms. "We must learn to better plan now that we have responsibilities—"

"Hush. Hush." I rubbed the worry furrows from her brow. "With your sex made safe once more, I claim what was robbed from me earlier." Our first misunderstanding a thing of the past, I savored her lips at last, and for a brief instant, we entered our own universe. "Heaven blessed us with you, my angel," I murmured.

"And what of you?" she murmured back. "A man brave enough to attack a gallows tree? A man who can talk to wolves?"

"You heard?"

"Of course, I heard. Even through the silent clamor of my prayers. Saw, too. Never will I forget—"

"*God save us, what now?*"

I whirled at something nipping my shoulder.

"*Blackspur.* So. I be not the only jealous fellow about. Or hungry one, either." I reluctantly released my sparrow. "We must move our patient. Blackspur has need of the bed for his breakfast!"

THIRTEEN

Father William's little book of hours—and
Christa's, too, her gift from Brother Thomas—
contained more than prayers and calendars.
Matched to each month of the year was also the
image of its astrological sign. Were not both nobil-
ity and clergy mad about astrology? Did not they
have horoscopes cast based on the exact moment of
their coming into the world? Such always made
much of the felicitous conjunctions of moon and
stars. . . . Aye, even my father oft had reminded
me that I was born in the twentieth hour of the
great Feast of the Epiphany, under the sign of
Aquarius. Aquarius was the water carrier, and as
January's heavens burst open upon us, I began to
rue this symbol of my birth.

Rain atop snow made the way hard even for
Blackspur. Then there was me, struggling alongside
him near up to my thighs in the muck. I glanced

forlornly from beneath my dripping hood at Christa and Max astride Blackspur's back. Verily, my horse was a grand and noble beast, yet never had I seen any his equal taking on three riders. Young Max had vehemently protested usurping my place, but while the fever still be on him . . .

I hacked and spat. As the lad was daily drenched and chilled, his cure lay not in sight. Neither were these weathers playing fair by me—I, who'd never had a sick day save from Otto's lash. Still more, there was the matter of my nearly emptied purse, never mind my misconceived quest—

> *Under the linden,*
> *On the heather,*
> *For us two a bed there was—*

"Christa!" Through the lashing rain, she'd unaccountably burst into song. "Christa, in God's holy name—"

"In God's holy name would I bring some joy to this misbegotten day. Some joy back into our lives. We are forgetting how to live, Conrad!"

I threw up my arms, bespattering her with mud. "What would you have? *Christ's sorrow!* I do all that is possible within me—" Whereupon I burst into a prodigious fit of coughing. Beside me, Blackspur halted in sympathy. Unbending from the fit at last, I looked again upon Christa, upon Max wanly clinging to her back. Already I missed the lad's outrageous tongue. Quest be damned. More important concerns bedeviled me. "If I could stop the rain! If I could find shelter warm enough, dry enough to bring us health—"

"Dearest Conrad." Christa reached cold fingers to caress my cheek. "No one could ask more than what you give. Now is it left to me to offer what I can give."

She broke into song again. But this time it was the Te Deum.

> *Holy God, we praise Thy Name,*
> *Mighty God, we bow before Thee—*

"Blackspur . . ." As he seemed the sole member of our party still in full possession of his wits, I turned to my horse in complaint. "Blackspur, can the Holy God see through the dark clouds He's chosen to shroud us with? Can the Mighty God hear through the icy rain He pours down upon us?"

My horse snorted. At God, or my lack of faith? Yet as Christa's hymn of praise strengthened, the steep road widened under our feet and broke through the hulking forest. Blackspur forced his strength, slowly gaining on the mountain's rise. I doggedly toiled next him till we came to its top. Sagged against Blackspur, eyes closed, fighting for the breath within me.

"Conrad! Look!"

I shielded my eyes from the driving rain and only then noted that it was no longer driving. It came still, but gently. Made the leap of faith and opened them fully. . . .

Below lay a valley. Nestled within was a town. Standing protectively over all from a cliff's peak beyond was a fortress.

"A castle!" Christa cried.

"Aye." I would not voice what that could mean. *Shelter. Food. Work.* Instead, I nudged Blackspur, and we carefully picked our way down the mountain.

Under a washy rainbow, our bedraggled party entered the town's square to find a procession wending its way toward the church. I caught at a straggler. "God be with you, good sir. Can you tell me what place this is?"

"Why, Kronach of the Frankenwald, of a cert!"

I pointed at the imposing stone castle towering over us. "And that?"

"Where are you from, man, not knowing the reputation of Fortress Rosenberg?"

I shrugged apologetically. "And the procession?"

He tugged his sleeve from my grasp and was away, crying "For the Feast of the Epiphany!"

"No more questions!" Christa begged from above. "To be traveling on a feast day is suspicious enough."

"Who knew it to be such?" I shot back.

"Especially the great Feast of the Epiphany—"

"Who knew it to be my birth day?" I laughed.

"Conrad! You are *sixteen?*"

"Aye, should I live through the day."

At which intelligence Max shook himself from his torpor, loosing his tongue in the process.

"Christ's nails and thorns! Sixteen be all? I thought sure you be reaching for Methuselah's record—"

My sparrow turned to knock upon his pate. "There's one for your blasphemy, young Max. It's time you were learning to better guard your speech. . . . And another for playing so lightly with your patron!"

Yet her blows were gentle. Max received them as gifts and proceeded to prattle all the way through Kronach's narrow streets.

"I'll not be long in catching up with Conrad. By my troth, I have nine years already . . . mayhap even ten?" He began counting on his fingers. Three he struck off. "Baby years don't signify." The fourth he held lovingly. "This year did Fader give me my first hammer and taught me to beat upon his anvil." The fifth he studied, then buried within his other fist. "This year did the Second Pest take Mutter."

The words pierced my heart. Young Max and I shared a common past. The *unthinkable*—another burst of the Great Plague—had occurred barely more than a decade after its first fury took *my* mother. I raised a hand of comfort to him, but Christa had already turned with a hug.

Max bravely shook loose. Found his sixth, seventh, and eighth fingers. "These years did I pump the bellows for our forge." He stared at the ninth finger, then shoved both hands within his cloak. The counting stopped. But I was already leading Blackspur up the slick, climbing way of the waiting mountain to the gray towers of Fortress Rosenberg.

✳ ✳ ✳

Blackspur clattered across the moat's drawbridge as far as the open gatehouse—and two liveried guards blocking our way with crossed halberds.

"Halt!"

As we were already as halted as was possible, I awaited their next pronouncement.

"What seek you in Lord Manfred's stronghold?"

"Peace be with you and all within!" I yanked off my hood, jangled my ass's ears, and gave them a sweeping bow—which truly was all I had within me at the moment. "I and my troupe of players seek audience with your great lord. We would make him merry this holy Feast of the Epiphany!"

"Pah!" exclaimed one. "Never did I see such sorry excuse for entertainers. What think you, Lucas?"

Lucas spat his disdain. "E'en a cat would ne'er drag them in."

Upon which, Christa lowered her hood, tossed her damp locks, and began to sing.

> *Sixty ladies rode their way*
> *Gracious and gay as the bird on the*
> > *tree,*
> *And never a knight in that company.*
> *Falcon on hand those ladies ride,*
> *On hawking bent, by the riverside—*

Seeing first what only now I spied, my nightingale had sent her voice flowing around the guards, through the gate, to the inner curtain beyond—where between keep and fortress walls a fine lady walked, airing a hawk upon her arm. I watched her graceful progress pause. Watched the several companions behind mince to a stop in unison. Held my breath till Christa's golden voice—and inspired choice of song—turned her toward us.

"Guards! Who comes here?"

Lucas and his comrade near skewered each other in their attempts to fawn upon the lady.

I stepped forward. Offered a far more elegant bow. "Conrad the Good, my lady, Christof the Fair, and Max of the Second Chance. Poor wandering fools and minstrels seeking your beneficence in return for our humble skills."

The lady frowned on me. "I pray your performance be better than your appearance." She waited for the titters of the women behind to cease. "Yet that one's voice . . ."

My nightingale silenced her song to speak. "But give us a little warmth and food, my lady, and our feathers will dry as fine as yon hawk's. Then may you watch us swoop and soar."

She arched a single eyebrow but nodded at a guard. "Take them to the kitchen. My lord may welcome a novelty for this evening's feast."

Praise God, Lord Manfred's cook was more hospitable than his lady.

"Merciful Heaven! What's to be done with these poor souls afore vespers?" She wiped floury hands on the voluminous apron swaddling her equally voluminous girth to raise a huge wooden spoon like a general. "Dirk! Ladle out some good, hot pottage. Maria! Fetch dry garments, then see to drying these." She eyed Max. "Soon as ever this lad's been fed and dosed, put him to bed with the warming pans."

Her attention turned next on me.

"Fie!" The spoon shook threateningly. "It takes a fool to be roaming these mountains in January. Know you not that Epiphany rains be like the coming of the Three Wise Kings to the Christ child? Their gifts and homage were but a respite afore the exile to Egypt. These rains are but a respite afore the second coming of the snows. And come they will, like to the wicked fury of Herod himself!"

I cringed beneath her spoon and beetled brows, till Blackspur saved me—nudging his head through the half-open door of the kitchen.

"Albrecht! Unload this great creature and see him to the stables and his own dinner!"

Sinking onto a bench, I sighed. "Thanks. Many thanks. You have been our salvation."

Cook plunked a steaming bowl before me. "Keep your thanks and gather your strength. You'll be needing it for his lordship."

Christa caught my eyes above the steam of her own bowl. Her silent question mirrored my own.

Had we stumbled on a lord worse than Otto?

✳ ✳ ✳

Dirk the Kitchen Boy dragged me from out the grasp of a deathlike sleep.

"Make haste, good fool! Even now Cook sends the cranes to Lord Manfred and Lady Afra's table!"

I gave my thanks as he scurried off, then crawled from beneath my share of the lambskin. Steadied myself against the tiny chamber's wall for a moment, trying to clear my head. Christa and Max slept on, so peaceful I barely had heart to waken them. Yet waken them I must. I reached first for Christa.

"Time to earn our supper, my thrush."

"Conrad?" One blink and she was aware, throwing off the blanket entire, exposing the lad, too. "Only look upon him," she paused to murmur.

I was looking. He was curled round the tambourine on which I'd spent the better part of my gold in the last town but one. Another hungry town, hoarding coins useless for filling stomachs. Max rasped hollowly and clutched his drum tighter.

"Let him sleep." I tucked the lambskin snugly over him. "We'll work together again, just the two of us."

Christa gave me a kiss. "I will follow your lead. Always."

I jammed on my fool's cap with a smile. "Unless you think of a better way first."

We entered the banqueting hall on the tail end of the progress of cranes. And it was a true progress. A herald clad in scarlet—bearing Lord Manfred's family device of two horizontal white stripes surrounding a fiercely taloned hawk's claw—was at its head, rallying all with the call of his long trumpet. Following him came eight servants in matching tunics groaning under their platters of crane. I fear my mouth must have hung agape at the sight, for Christa gave me a prod. I shut it, but wonder remained. First there be the cost of crane itself. Only once had I seen it on Otto's table. Next there be the sheer number. Lastly there be the presentation: Feathers had been gilded and reapplied to the roasted flesh. A necklace of pearls adorned each bird's neck below beady eyes and polished beaks.

I hesitated at the entrance to the great raftered room. How could my modest skills, my simple pipe, compete with such show?

"*Courage,*" my beloved whispered into my ear. Then did she give me a shove.

I fell into a handspring, then another. Felt the naturalness of the motions returning to me. Felt the food and sleep strengthening me. Changed midleap into a cartwheel. Thus did I travel the length and breadth of the brightly torch-lit hall. Thus did I note the number and variety of hunting birds perched beside their masters and mistresses, the rich hunting tapestries adorning the walls. Thus did I careen to the very dais that held Lord Manfred of Rosenberg, that held his lady and most honored retainers, that held the sinful extravagance of crane, that held—

I twirled to a final stop.

116

"Ho! What have we here? Another fool, I fear! Yet be he mighty of wit, or merely a chit? A flea-scratching, thump-stumping, idiot twit?"

Balanced atop a throne of cushions between Lord Manfred and his lady, Afra, was a humpbacked dwarf, placidly sucking on a string of pearls dangling from his drooling mouth.

FOURTEEN

Though Otto had not the means to hawk, I was not ignorant of the sport's appeal. Had not Vincent de Beauvais's encyclopedia included an entry on falconry? To buy and train a worthy bird required falconers and assistants, and mews far better built than any serf's hut. Requiring great expenditures of time and money only heightened the sport's attraction. Did the very act not assume high status? And was it not said that as a falconer lures back his straying hawk with raw meat, just so Christ wins sinners back to grace by showing them His wounds? Yet Manfred of Rosenberg's court had little interest in either Christ's grace or Christ's wounds.

Of an instant, the din of the great hall stilled. From the corner of my eye, I caught another procession of servers freezing in their steps. Spied courtiers reaching nervously to smooth the feathers of their perched birds. Only then did I strengthen my stance before the dais, defiantly shake my bells—and look upon Lord Manfred of Rosenberg.

He set down his knife, dabbled in a waiting water bowl, then carefully patted fingers and lips dry with a fine linen napkin. As the silence surrounding us grew painful, he finally turned to me—and skewered me with his eyes. Hooded like a bird of prey they were, and *cold,* colder than the Ninth Circle of Hell. I struggled from out their frigid depths to study the stony face beneath a skull smooth and hairless as an egg . . . joined to the neck of a bull, its veins throbbing rage the face would never reveal. My heart pounded within me as he raised a hand—

Mercy. The nail of its last finger was long and sharp as any eagle's talon.

—and lovingly caressed his dwarf's carefully waved hair. "Grock . . ."

Manfred's voice was soft, the voice of a parent to his favored child. Yet there was a sinister undertone that curdled my blood.

"What is the Rosenberg motto, Grock?"

The imbecile dropped the pearls, squinched his eyes, and in a high, piping voice parroted, "*Contun-de-re impor-tuni . . . ta-tem*"—a pause to pound upon his head for remembrance—"*Proter-ere . . . igno-min-i . . . am!*"

Crush insolence. Trample dishonor.

Pleased by his performance, he nodded to himself, then

snatched up the pretty things and popped them back into his mouth.

"Well spoken, but you are not yet finished, my fine Grock." His lordship's hand slipped from his toy's head to grasp the back of its neck. "What say you to this challenge?"

I watched as Manfred's clasp tightened. As Grock swallowed the pearls in surprise. Eyes bulging, he turned red . . . then purple. Still the iron grip held. But another moment and this pitiful plaything would be dead. There was no choice. Scattering gilded cranes to the wind, I leaped upon the dais, shoved a boot against the poor dwarf's chest, thrust my hand into his mouth—

"All due respect, my lord"—a quick nod toward his master—"but false honor will soon find this knave in his grave!"

A kick, a tug—and pearls emerged—along with a mighty chuff of air and the remainder of the contents of Grock's stomach. I knelt before him, yanking his head by the hair to keep his nose from his own vomit. Counting the gilded feathers swimming in his slime.

Manfred spoke at last. "Steward! Clean up this filth! Bathe Grock! At once!" Those hooded eyes turned on me. "Guards! Escort this fool to my dungeons!"

"Nay!" Grock whimpered. Gathering his few scattered wits, he raised his heavy head and embraced me in his stubby arms. Gave me a fetid kiss. "Grock choke. No air. See black. See *Hell*." He fished in the puddle for the pearls and thrust them at me. "You good. You—"

"Conrad." I smiled, accepting the gift.

The smile he returned was heart-wrenching. "Conrad save Grock. Grock *love* Conrad."

A pained sniff came from Lady Afra as she attempted to keep the spreading puddle from her finery. "Fie, my lord, cannot the steward move himself more quickly? My new gown . . . and"—she raised slim, bejeweled fingers to the hooded bird uneasily coiling and uncoiling its claws on the standing perch next to her—"the stench is upsetting my Precious."

As the belated steward rushed forward to save his job and possibly his skin, I sank back on my haunches to await Manfred's final decision as to *my* disposition. How much more hellish could his dungeon be than this very table?

He sliced his talon like a knife through the weave of the tablecloth before him. Once. Twice. Then looked upon me again. His lips curled. "Since Grock has taken a fancy to you, you shall have a reprieve. We shall see how well you can keep me entertained." He waved away the hovering guards and roared, "Chamberlain!"

A harried, gray-bearded old fellow jumped from the last place on the dais.

"My lord?"

"See that this . . . this *Conrad?* . . ."

I did a backward flip from the table's top, landing nicely balanced on the balls of my feet. Made a fine bow. Too fine for Manfred of Rosenberg. "Conrad *the Good,* my lord. Simple fool for Christ's sake. Mine to give and yours to take."

The eyes turned to ice. "Time will tell. In the interim,

Chamberlain, I will not have a shabby fool in attendance upon me. See to it."

Thus dealt with, I was no longer any of his concern. Breath returned, and with it strength enough to cartwheel out the hall after the rapidly disappearing Christa and Grock. Yet my pardon did not come with joy. Neither did the sounds now tentatively refilling the great hall. Under such a master and mistress, relief was but a scant reprieve from fear.

Christa found me packing our saddlebags in the tiny chamber.

"Wake Max," I ordered. "And roll up the lambskin—"

She caught my hands. Stilled their labors. "You would leave in the dark of night?"

"I would flee while my sixteen years yet have chance to become seventeen. Sooner would I take on a hundred more wolf-filled forests than remain in this accursed place."

"Conrad, Conrad." She bent to hug me, then pulled away wrinkling her nose. "You smell of natural fool."

"The rains will wash me clean again." I buckled a bag and stretched for the other.

"Nay." She pushed it away. "Only come with me for a breath of fresh air. It will clear your head remarkably."

"Now be not the time for games, sparrow!"

She reached out again. "Please."

With muttered imprecations did I follow her from the chamber, down dank corridors of stone, to the heat of a kitchen too harried with the preparation of sweetmeats to note our passing, through the door, and into the courtyard.

"Christ's blood!"

Must I now do penance for Herod's ancient sins as well? Falling to my knees, I cried my anguish to the Heaven sending this new cross for me to bear. Pounded the ground. Howled. All for naught. The snow fell heavy and hard. It would keep falling thus and so.

Christa knelt beside me. "Winter will end, Conrad. It must end. We will survive."

I buried my head between her banded breasts. And there she comforted me as the snow silently cloaked us in white.

FIFTEEN

"As snow in summer, and as rain in harvest, so honor is not seemly for a fool." Thus is it written in Proverbs. The same chapter also says, "A whip for the horse, a bridle for the ass, and a rod for the fool's back." I do most vehemently take exception to both verses. Manfred of Rosenberg did not.

"Conrad, Conrad! Come and play!"

Grock pummeled us awake with bunched fists the next morn. Christa shifted sleepily in my arms and blinked up at him through a shaft of light falling from the arrow loop.

"Pretty lady!" He bent to reverently touch her hair.

From the lips of children and fools. I sighed and extricated myself. Rest within my beloved's embrace had calmed my premonitions of disaster, and now must I make accommodations to our second winter entrapment. "Can you keep a secret, Grock?"

He solemnly crossed his heart.

"Christof is a lady in hiding, in *disguise*, and *no one* must know."

"Princess?"

"Aye." Why not? "Hiding from wicked lords." In truth.

"*Oooh*. Grock protects. Always!"

Whereupon Max rolled out from under the blanket's far side. Squinted through his thatch of hair—

"Christ's love! You've gone and rescued another poor beggar! Could've waited till I was awake and helping!"

"Conrad's boy!" Grock leaped upon him with a slobbering kiss, and they proceeded to tussle like puppies.

Thus did Grock insinuate himself into our family. It was not a hardship. What God had denied him in intelligence He'd replaced with sweetness. Treated as a human instead of a *toy*, he blossomed. As we spoke with him, his speech broadened. As he ate with us, he learned both control and almost civilized table manners.

"Here now—" Max put a stop to Grock's third helping during a kitchen meal. "Don't want to be a glutton, do you?"

"What *glutton*?" Grock asked, spitting half his overfilled mouthful at all within range.

Max stuffed his own mouth, puffed out his cheeks, and mimed Grock. "Don't look nice, do it?" he spluttered. "Makes you fat and stupid, too, all that food." He swallowed the lump with difficulty. Took a deep breath. "You wants to be lean and mean, like me. Right, Conrad?"

The mirth I tried to hide near choked me. "Without a doubt."

Next to Grock, Christa smiled a gentle smile and applied a napkin to his face. "The knight who protects me must be shiny and clean."

He snatched the cloth. "Grock learn."

Just so had my small troupe expanded yet again. Now we clustered near the banqueting hall's entrance, awaiting our summons to perform. Like a proud master about to send forth his apprentices for their journeyman trials, I examined each. A scarlet silken tunic set Christa off well. Her golden curls gleamed with brushing, her eyes sparkled with thoughts of the challenge ahead, and—hedging our bets—a codpiece swelled her tights. . . . Behind her, Max, with his fever dosed and slept away at last, clutched his tambourine. His threadbare garments had been exchanged for scarlet as well. But it was Grock—loving all things shiny—who had contrived the gilding of Max's iron neckband. And young Max exhibited it like some badge of honor—verily, like a pagan Hun well girded for battle. . . . Grock was dressed in matching scarlet costume. He'd been out of favor with his lord and lady since the "disgusting" pearl incident, so I took a calculated risk with his inclusion. For himself, Grock took no notice of the politics involved. Nor did he show signs of missing his old patrons. In the course of our weeklong preparations, already he'd become slimmer, more alert. Now he rocked from foot to foot, holding to his lips his instrument of choice—a small brass horn—lest he miss a moment of his triumphal entry.

As for me . . . I shook my new scarlet fool's cap with its bright yellow felt cockscomb. The fit was more perfect since I'd surrendered to a haircut—"Nay!" Christa had screeched at the chamberlain's barber. "But trim, not shave! Only size the cap's cloth larger!"—yet my ears were unaccustomed to the alien tones of the new bells. Gilded brass and much-prized they were, from the foundries of Dordrecht. I sighed. My old bells sang more sweetly. The remainder of my costume: one leg of scarlet, one of white; soft scarlet leathern slippers; a doublet of diagonal scarlet and white stripes. And more bells, clanging from every knuckle and joint. Another sigh. I owned true motley at last. Why, then, did I feel like a peacock in mating season? More to the point: how long might I be given grace to wear it?

Manfred's flunkies had tripped over themselves in decorating us, as if for roasting and the platter. Beneath their solicitude lay fear. Fear blanketed all of Fortress Rosenberg, save Cook's kitchen. "Ach, he's always been the bloody-minded one, but shorter memories forget its usefulness," she'd said to me only this afternoon. "Was it not Lord Manfred himself who swept down on the Free Company of raiders set to plunder and rape all of Kronach but three years past? Like the avenging fist of God he was! Saved my good sister and her three virgin daughters from a fate worse than death." Her wooden spoon swooped in approval. "His lordship only pines for a proper war," Cook concluded. " 'Tis a pity that crusade to Hungary against the Turks failed last summer. Needs someone to sink his talons into, he does."

"Conrad. *Conrad!*" Christa yanked me from my thoughts. "We are beckoned!"

Piping my pipe, I led forth my little band. To a sprightly tune from Christa, Max jigged circles about us, tapping his tambourine in good time. It had taken considerable patience to train him so, when his natural instinct be to pound it like hammer to anvil. Completing the musical prologue, Grock blew upon his horn. Only one note could he achieve, but that he achieved with passion. So did we parade about the banqueting hall, bringing quickly hidden smiles and chuckles from Lord Manfred's court. To the very foot of the dais facing the hall we came, bowed in unison, then one-two-three!

Christa knelt for the base of a pyramid. . . .

Max scrambled upon her back. . . .

Grock climbed both to balance atop Max's shoulders.

A final blast from Grock's horn sent me into a quick, jingling flip next to them. Laughing in pride for my troupe, I spread my arms—

"To bore do we four all abhor. Your mighty lordship, we implore—pray tell us what you wish explored. Standing ready hearts to pour, we fain would not be quite ignored!"

I awaited the hall's applause. The hall awaited Manfred. Very carefully did he extract his knife from the roast before him and lay it down. The washing ritual should come next. . . . He spoke instead, his ominously low voice reverberating through the hush and setting my human pyramid to teetering.

"More than a week and this is all you bring me? A beardless youth whose voice must soon break without timely castration, a ragamuffin with no discernible gifts, and my own Grock schooled to pierce my skull with that infernal noise?"

So, he would exercise his talons this night on me and mine.

Dropping my arms and smile, I made another bow, then threw my gauntlet in his face. "These innocents should sparèd be; the fight lies sole twixt thee and me."

"As you say." He snapped his fingers, and my troupe toppled back to earth and disappeared in ignominy. *Then* did he reach for the rose-scented waters of his bowl, proffered by Lady Afra in malicious expectation. As he went through the motions, how I did long for Otto's honest choler. . . . At last, Lord Manfred completed his preparations and set his wicked eyes upon me.

"If it is to be a challenge, it must be a fair one. As I cannot expect a mere fool to meet me in the jousts with sharpened lance, we shall see instead how sharp your intellect be." His lips made their little twist. "My scholar has been at task to answer several questions for me. It will be an amusement to learn what wisdom an *artificial* fool might bring to these queries."

Another bow. "*Riddle-dee-dee*, your *will* be a fait accompli. Yet what gain *I* by my good answers to thee?"

He reached beneath his fur-lined robe for a purse and

tossed it on the table. It landed with the heavy clink of gold. Next he ordered, "Oswald the Alchemist!"

I turned to watch a bony, stooped, long-bearded fellow shuffle from the very farthest table of the hall. His demeaning position told me he was nowhere near the discovery of transmuting gold from base metals. What questions might he have for me? How could he and Manfred possibly expect a wise answer from one who had never studied philosophy or the composition of metals or the stars?

Oswald finally halted before the dais, looking very uncomfortable, indeed. He peered at me, then Manfred, then tugged his cap more firmly over his head. For his efforts, its greasy point drooped worse than my ass's ears. Cleared his throat as if speech were a thing he rarely used. . . .

"M'lord—"

"Get on with it, Oswald," Manfred rasped. "Ask the first question!"

More shuffling. "Of matters theological, arithmetical, or—"

"A question! Any question!"

Shoulders rose and fell in a long-practiced shrug of defeat. "Kindly tell us, then, Master Fool . . . from the beginning of God's Creation until today, how many days have passed?"

I flipped into a handstand, the better for the blood to flow into my head. Paced thus back and forth before the dais. Back and forth. All I could think of was Blackspur, and a counting trick I once taught him. For some reason known only to himself, he always refused counting past the number seven. Just curled up his hoof and gave me the eye. . . . *Seven*.

"Ho!" I was on my feet again. "The answer is clear as clear can be! *Seven*, by holy Heaven! There is Sunday"—I pointedly counted on my fingers, twirling between Manfred and the hall—"followed by Monday . . . next Tuesday . . . then Wednesday . . . Thursday . . . Friday . . . and Saturday!" A shake of my bells. "Thus God ordained from the very first day, and who are we to say Him nay?"

Upon which pronouncement, I jingled into a cross-legged heap upon the rush-covered floor, cocked head upon palm upon elbow, and silently dared Manfred to dispute me.

He did not.

Instead, he unfurled *both* his talons and sliced his wrath into the cloth before him. I would not be the castle seamstress tasked to keep the Lord of Rosenberg in table linens. When the throbbing in his neck calmed, he reached for his purse and tossed a coin at me. As I snatched it from the air, he was already commanding, "The next question!"

"Forsooth, m'lord—" Oswald tried in protest.

I began sympathizing with the old man. A jest was a jest, but my mischievous answer did naught but bring contumely upon his life's work.

"Ask!"

Oswald the Alchemist lowered his head in shame. "Where, Master Fool—"

"*Louder*," Manfred prodded. "So all the court might hear."

His head jerked up, and a tear began flowing from a wrinkled eye. A tremble of impotent protest ran through his body. Yet he raised his voice. "There has been much dispute among scholars as to the correct center of the world. Be it Jerusalem, where Our Lord was crucified; or Rome, the proper seat of Holy Mother Church since Peter himself; or Avignon, where the pope does sit in splendid exile—"

"Enough!" Manfred cried. "I'll not have aspersions cast upon His Holiness Urban!"

Oswald cowered, muttering, "None meant, m'lord, none at all, yet the point needs pursuing—"

Past time for putting the old man out of his misery. Springing to my feet, I shook my ass's ears, grinned like the idiot I was meant to be, and proclaimed, "Spread but a tape clear round the world from where I stand"—I formed a ball with one fist and ran an imaginary line around its circumference—"*here* lies the center . . . in Lord Manfred's lands!"

This answer did his lordship approve. He barked an odd bark of a laugh, followed by convulsions from his hall full of retainers. Then did he toss me *three* golden coins from his purse.

"A last question!"

The mirth died as if sliced by a knife.

Oswald made effort to gather the tattered shreds of his dignity. Asked the final question: "Why does a bird fly?"

I turned to study Manfred's court: coiffed women in their Sunday best of samite and miniver; courtiers of every ilk, ready to prostrate themselves before the Lord of Rosenberg and his lady wife; and hawks—everywhere hooded and jessed hawks. Verily, this was the simplest question of all. So did I answer it simply.

"To be *free*."

"*Guards!*" roared Manfred.

As I was stripped of my motley, as Lord Manfred descended from his dais to accept the whip thrust at him . . . all I could think was, *Fool! You've overreached. Again.*

SIXTEEN

If folly were a pain, how you would hear me howl.

The parapet walk was deserted at midnight. From my height atop Blackspur's back, the valley of the Frankenwald spread below me, buried in snow. Beyond lay more mountains, smothered in snow. Were I lord of this fortress, mayhap the sight would give me pride. Instead, I shivered with the latest blast of wind and bent to study the hourglass I'd set between the outer wall's crenellations. Brushed from it the snow that had accumulated since my last round. Most of the sand had trickled to the bottom. Close enough. I upended it so the process might begin anew, then turned toward the castle keep, toward the corner tower where I knew Lord Manfred of Rosenberg lay sleepless, awaiting my response to the strange duel we two played.

"*Cock-a-doodle-doo!*" I crowed through the snowy night.

Blackspur shook his mane and snorted.

"Your contempt is perfect, my friend," I assured him. "Would I could snort with such aplomb! But come now, we have an hour's respite before this cock must crow again."

I led him to the warmth of the stables, where he clomped past sleeping stableboys—

"By Christ's foe!" one made complaint. "Can you not give it a rest?"

"Place the saddle on the right horse," I addressed the bundled lump. "I do but follow our lord's pleasure."

"Aye, try saddling *that* horse, and I be out there walking the night with you!"

This, then, was Manfred's revenge for my too honest foolery. "Why waste you in the dungeons?" he'd said after venting his spleen on my already scarred back. "I shall put your cockscomb to better use!" Now was I become the castle rooster, doomed to crow every hour upon the hour through the long darkness—from one hour past compline to one hour before prime and sunrise. The only friend I'd gained from the sentence was Joachim the Bellringer. For the first time in his life was he able to sleep through the blackest hours.

"Here is your stall, Blackspur," I murmured. "Thank you for your good company."

"What thanks have you for me, Sir Rooster?"

"Christa!" I spun toward her, arms wide with hunger.

"Nay." She ignored them. "First I must see to your poor back."

"Again," I sighed as I knelt upon the bed of straw she'd prepared and began slipping off cloak and tunic. "When will you begin losing patience with this wretched fool?"

"Only when this wretched fool concedes defeat to Lord Manfred and his like." She pushed me flat and eased the shirt from my back. "My only wish is that I might have come sooner, but you know it has been forbidden me." Her fingers blindly studied the contours of my back as though it were a well-known map. "Yet the bleeding is finished. Mayhap cold helps the healing."

I groaned under her touch as she spread ointments. "Tell that to my frozen fingers, toes, and nose." When no further sympathy was offered, I asked what I'd been longing to know these last dark days since my fall from grace, since my separation from loved ones. "How goes it with you, sparrow? With my troupe, while Manfred's guards keep me jailed the livelong days?"

My dove snickered. "Grock was heartbroken by his lord-ship's disdain till Max took it upon himself to teach him a *second* note upon the horn. Whereupon Max discovered *he*, *too*, could play the horn. Whereupon they began brawling for possession of the horn. . . ."

I smiled into the straw pillowing my face. "And how did you end the dispute?"

Her fingers stilled. "The chamberlain accomplished that, arriving as he did with the barber-surgeon at his back."

"What—"

"Sent by *Lady Afra*, to dispossess me of my 'manhood.'

It seems she has been brooding over the expected loss of my voice—"

"*What?*" I jerked around. "By all the saints—"

"*Hush.*" She clapped fingers over my mouth. "You'll wake the stableboys again."

"Devil take the stableboys!" I yanked away and half up.

"Conrad." She caught me. "I had protection in full. My young knights fell upon the chamberlain and barber both—beating, biting, and kicking till they were gone in haste from our chamber."

"But what of the next attempt? If you do be discovered—"

"Blessed Conrad"—her arms tightened—"contain yourself. We have new allies in Cook and all her kitchen staff. Indeed, in much of the castle's good folk. In speaking of the forbidden, you've moved their sympathies. They are ready to do battle should the alarm be given."

"Setting them within Manfred's wrath as well."

I groaned and bowed my head upon her shoulder. My fault again. My pride would be the ruin of us all. When would I learn to judge what wisdom a lord stood ready to receive? When would I accept that *freedom* was the most frightening word to fall upon the ears of the ruling class?

She cradled me. Giggled. "Could you have seen the barber flee with bowl upon his head—"

"Christa, Christa." I reached under her tunic, under her shirt. Searched for the solace to be found beneath the band across her chest. "How can we escape this accursed place?"

She fumbled for my hand. Held it close to her, yet not

close enough. "Have you measured the snow, Conrad? The road down to Kronach is closed. Entombed by avalanche. Manfred must rely upon his stored provisions to feed his castle—and already Cook has struck two courses from this night's supper."

I sought her lips since all else was withheld. My kiss, too, she refused.

"I must go back or be discovered. Manfred's spies sneak into our little chamber at odd hours. And is it not near time for the cock to crow again?"

"Curses on Manfred!" I began collecting my discarded garments. "May he and his talons and his monstrous family motto all be blasted to the Last Circle of Hell!"

Christa did not dispute me. Instead, she stretched for my lips and gave me my kiss at last. "As soon as ever it is possible, I will return."

Despite all, I would she left with a smile lighting her face. I tipped her chin. "See that you cling to your *manhood* till then."

By God's grace was my cell aboveground. Its remarkable attributes were sung incessantly by my two jailers—none other than Lucas and his cohort, Nicholas, relieved of gate-house duty by Lord Winter.

"This betters the dungeons, eh, Lucas?"

From where I lay upon my thin mat, sending puffs of white breath toward the sliver of sky offered by my arrow loop, I could hear him beating arms against body as he paced through the drafty corridor. The open grate high in the door also gave me access to the reply.

"Forsooth. It pains me descending those slimy steps. And the rats—"

"Aye. Bigger than dogs some of them be." Nicholas hawked and spat. "God forbid we be after hunting them for our suppers soon."

I could almost see Lucas's shrug. "As long as the ale barrels flow, I am content. By my troth, a cup for our warming would not now go amiss." A pause. "You there! Halt! This way is barred to all!"

"Stay, Lucas. It be only his lordship's idiot. What cheer, Grock?"

That roused me. My first visitor in two long weeks of confinement in this thankless cell. My only visitor . . . if he was successful. I waited for the heavy, rolling footsteps to close in on my guards. Listened to the heaving gasps for air, then—

"Grock *love* Conrad. Grock *see* Conrad!"

"Nay, it be forbidden!"

Whereupon my little dwarf friend began to wail most hideously.

"Stop that caterwauling, you stunted runt of a numbskull—"

"No more! Unhand him, Lucas. He belongs to Lord Manfred!"

Grock upped his volume.

"Enough, enough! What harm can it do? Give the deformity his wish!"

Grinning, I waited for the bar to be raised. Waited for the hinges to creak in protest . . . then Grock flew into my arms. I hugged him till the door was shut again. Then did I pry him from me with a smile.

"You bring news, Grock?"

Winking an enormous wink, he retrieved a huge purse hidden beneath his tunic and like a magician proceeded to bring forth wonders.

He giggled and whispered conspiratorially. "Cook loves Conrad." Two well-stuffed meat pies. "Shoemaker loves Conrad." A new set of leathern juggling balls! "Max loves Conrad." My pipe. "Princess loves Conrad." My parchment and writing tools! "Bellringer loves Conrad." Ho, a flagon of wine. "And Grock loves Conrad!" Reaching beneath his tunic yet again, he carefully unwound what had been wrapped around his body. A woolen blanket!

"Grock, dear Grock. How I do love you, too." Another hug and I took him by the shoulders and looked into his eyes. "Is my Christa well? And Max?"

He solemnly nodded. "We play for kitchen. To . . . to . . ."

"Keep practicing your skills?"

"Aye. Only Princess sing at supper."

"No more barber visits?"

"Nay. We fight. We win. Grock and Max!"

I clasped his hand, man to man. "You are both fine warriors. Fine knights. Do you keep protecting my princess—"

The hinges began their creak, and I scurried to hide my booty.

"Out you come, Grock." Lucas's big red nose poked through the crack. "The fool needs his beauty sleep." A roar of mirth. "Got to be in fine feathers for his night's performance."

"Send my thanks and love to all," I whispered. "You are a splendid actor."

Another huge wink. "Grock keeps secrets."

As the massive door groaned shut behind him, Grock set up another great wail, till my jailers booted him down the corridor.

Then did I drape blanket around shoulders and launch into my feast. Stomach content, next came the testing of my juggling skills—neglected since gifting my last set of balls to Brother John. Truly, I'd forgotten how soothing it was to send the balls toward Heaven. Forgotten how the gestures always freed my mind to work in new ways. When my eyes lit upon the writing tools, I laughed. Should Grock visit again—should the castle staff still be warm to my plight—here were the means for an outrageous jest against Manfred!

Catching the balls, I spread open a clean sheet of parchment, took up my quill, and began to draw from memory. . . .

✳ ✳ ✳

It was Christa herself who brought the final device to me some two weeks hence. I was in the stables with Blackspur, currying him for the day to come. There was but one more hour to crow before I must deliver myself back into the hands of my jailers.

"Sparrow! Is it finished at last?"

She proudly displayed her parcel. "Wilfred the Carpenter just placed it in my hands, Conrad! The entire castle—well, the entire castle's staff—is early awake to hear the results. You have no idea how this has kept them smiling through the last dreadful days of Manfred's endless ill temper and winter's endless snows. Your sole voice has roused them. Your revenge becomes theirs as well—"

I stopped listening. Greedily did I tear open the sack to finger the wood's smoothness, to reach through the darkness for where I knew cogs and wheels lay in wait. I needed more light for my admiration. Needed to learn if I'd remembered well. *Would it work?*

"The night is clear." I tugged at Christa, then hoisted my fine jest—a jest fit to best Lord Manfred at last. "Come with me!"

Together we climbed the parapet wall to where the hourglass waited. Carefully clearing a stone block of snow, I set down the contrivance. Examined it more carefully by moonlight. Wilfred the Carpenter had lovingly polished each wooden wheel and gear. He'd oiled them well. . . . And here was a key for the winding. Here the string that set the works in motion. *Do I dare?*

142

I gulped for air like Grock. Turned the key. Once, twice, three times. Looked at my beloved. "Is it time?"

"Oh, Conrad. Nearly!"

She grabbed for my hand, and breathlessly we watched the final grains of sand slip through the hourglass's neck.

"Aye!" she cried.

I pulled the string. Wheels ground smoothly. . . .

"Cock-a-doodle-doo!"

Christa leaped into my arms. "It works!"

"Cock-a-doodle-doo!"

I stared at the machine through her embrace. "Methinks it works too well."

"Cock-a-doodle-doo!"

The grinding stopped. The cock was stilled. Across the outer ward, the mullioned window of Lord Manfred's tower chamber sprang open. His nightcapped head burst out.

"Come to me, dunceling. With bird."

SEVENTEEN

Endless toil may have been the punishment de-
creed by God Almighty after the Fall, but did not
this drudgery force mankind to sharpen its wits?
Left in Eden, would there be a plow? A wheel? An
alphabet? The threat of Lord Manfred's talons had
a similar effect. . . .

"Explain yourself, fool."

I stood boldly unrepentant in the candlelight of Manfred's square chamber, the innards of my rooster sitting in all their cogged glory upon his table.

" 'Twas meant in jest, your lordship, since crowing by night was grown stale."

He waved off my excuse. "Tell me how you *knew* to make it."

A shrug of worldly nonchalance. "In travels with my father, as a child, I came upon the great clock of Strasbourg

Cathedral. . . . Being but a lad, I was much taken by its crowing cock—"

"Can you make more?" he snapped. "Can you make a great clock for Fortress Rosenberg?"

I made a bow. Felt a trickle of sweat beginning to run down my spine through the chill. Boldness was no replacement for ignorance. Here lay peril. *Stand fast. Still did I hold the advantage.*

"If I am released from confinement. Released from my nightly duties. Given free use of your artisans—"

"Pah." He swept away these minor obstructions.

Another bow. "I can but try."

"*Trying* is not acceptable. Do so." With a single talon, Lord Manfred carefully scoured a new groove into his much-scarred tabletop. "*By Easter.*"

Mercy.

I collected my device and turned to leave.

"Also do you see that my servants make haste to add feathers to that cock's crow of yours!"

"As you wish, my lord."

I fled.

It was to the kitchen that I retreated, there to find the castle's staff in worried gathering. Upon sight of me safe, a low *huzzah* rose. My rooster was replaced by a cup of ale. . . .

I raised it. "Heartfelt thanks to thee! Our rooster crowed magnificently!"

"*Two times* too magnificently," someone grumbled.

"Fie! Have pity on the bird," Cook said. "He only re-played Saint Peter's betrayal for the sake of our souls' good."

Yet it was because of those last two crows that I and all surrounding me were in new hazard. I sought out Christa. There she stood, lounging next to the dangling chains and spits of the great open fireplace like some careless youth, with a sleepy Max and Grock at her feet. We caught each other's eyes. With her steadfast gaze fueling me anew, I raised my cup again.

"One crow or three, pleased his lordship be." I waited for the relief to set in. "Yet he gives us a new task, the which we must accomplish fast."

So did I explain our bidding. Paused for the idea to take hold. . . .

"*A great clock!*"

Reverence, nay *awe*, filled the room.

"Like to sacred cathedrals and noble cities—"

"In our own Fortress Rosenberg of the Frankenwald!"

"For *all* of us to admire!"

"Albrecht!" Cook ordered. "Bring out the bowls! Dirk! Heat the grill! Fat Tuesday as it is, we'll see in Lent—and our great clock—with a feast of pancakes!"

I needed sleep. Yet above all did I need Christa. Max and Grock having happily gorged on pancakes to near immobil-ity, they willingly collapsed into guard duty outside our tiny chamber. With the closing of its door, with privacy at last, I sank onto the lambskin and spread my arms wide for my dove. She flew into them as if our weeks of separation were naught. And there we clung till the memory of my latest folly overcame even the joy of her closeness.

"What to do?" I moaned. "Only forty days till Easter. Forty days to succeed. For a surety, it will be the *dungeons* this time, for I have no knowledge of the building of great clocks!"

"Forty-one." Christa smiled. "Tomorrow is Ash Wednesday. You yet have today, Shrove Tuesday, to rest and think." She pulled my head onto her lap, tugged off my fool's cap, and slowly began running fingers through my cropped hair. "How did you manage the rooster, Conrad?"

"I know not how to explain!"

"Having you back again, I have the patience to listen. Patience for anything so long as I may look upon you. Touch you."

"*Sparrow.*" For my beloved, I made effort to try. But where to begin? At the beginning, when I first became aware of my difference. I willed exhaustion away.

"Memory . . . is one of the greatest tools of a fool. Thanks be to Heaven, mine is sound . . . yet a little *unusual.* My father did say . . ." I closed my eyes in remembrance. Hans the Large appeared before me: huge in my child's mind, a proud smile creasing his broad beard. His words rose out of me. " 'Aye, you've been blessed with a special memory, son. Keep its mysteries hidden, like a priceless jewel, for few will comprehend. . . . And see you do use it for the good.' " I blinked up at Christa. "At first, I did not understand, but once I had my letters, the patterns became meaningful. Only to look upon the written word . . . to see but once the drawing of a thing . . ."

Her fingers gently stroked my temples, silently bidding me on. So soothing they were, easing the secret out from me.

"I cannot forget, Christa. Never! The pages of books—Dante's *Comedy*, Beauvais's *Speculum* . . . pictures I have seen. They float through my head . . . till I have need of them!"

She bent to kiss my brow. "It is a great gift."

"Is it? Just see what it has begun. In kindness to this curious child, my father did befriend the timekeeper of Strasbourg's clock—who spread wide his plans for me to look upon."

"You cannot remember the other pictures?"

"My only interest was the bird!" I reached for her. "What must I do?"

Another kiss. "For now, you must sleep. When you are well rested, then you must visit old Oswald for his advice."

"Oswald the Alchemist? After the scorn I placed upon his shoulders?"

"In humbleness will you visit him. With apologies—and with the drawings for your rooster. Lying within them must rest nearly everything necessary for the workings of a clock. If those wheels can be harnessed to a cock's crow, why cannot they be harnessed to time? He is wise enough to find these hidden things."

I stared up at my beloved. "No one is as wise—or kind—as you."

"Dearest Conrad, it comes easily with love."

So did she cosset me till I slept.

Never did I picture Conrad the Jester, Conrad the Fool, overseer of a great workshop. Yet in the waning days of that endless winter did I spend my folly chivying, begging, pleading. When all else failed did I juggle or leap or sing most atrociously. Anything to bring smiles, for a happy heart sped labor. Anything to achieve our purpose within the days of Lent. Anything to keep me from the slime and dog-rats of the dungeons. And working beside me was Oswald. His shoulders no longer stooped, for he'd found a goal infinitely more attainable than counting the days since Creation or turning dross to gold. He it was who put names to my rooster's mysterious cogs and wheels.

"It is self-evident."

This he'd said after a single glance at my plans, after I'd made my heartfelt apologies. I'd done so nervously—not from lack of sincerity, but because of the strange lair he hunched within like some half-blind mole. All was shadows under the squat, barrel-vaulted chamber secreted within the castle's lower depths. Monstrous shadows they were, surrounding smoking retorts and open books whose letters faded in the sulfurous reek. Yet Oswald's rheumy eyes were sympathetic.

"Fools and scholars hold much in common," he'd

admitted. "Both are destined to spend their talents on deaf ears." Reaching hungrily for my parchment, he weighed down the curled edges of the vellum with an assortment of beakers, then balanced spectacles upon his nose. Still he squinted through the lamplight dimly illuminating the long worktable.

"Four things are necessary for his lordship's clock," he proclaimed at last. "First is a source of power." He pointed to the weights I'd sketched. "Second is a gear to transmit the power." He stabbed at the image of a wheel and the thin rope wound round it, connected to the weights. "Third is the escapement"—another prod of gnarled finger—"to keep the power from exhausting itself too quickly. It controls the escape of power, the speed of the turning gears and wheels. With the addition of a pendulum, it makes the tick and the tock." Then he'd smiled through the wispy tangles of his beard. "The last thing we must add ourselves."

"What?"

"Why, a face on which time can be read!"

"Is it as easy as that?"

"As simple . . . and as difficult." He'd rubbed his hands together and begun to mumble. "Size must be taken into account, and proper calibration. . . ."

Now was the workshop like nothing so much as a swarming beehive. Wilfred the Carpenter and his assistants were sawing and measuring wood. Grock squatted on the floor next to the stonemasons, happily bashing at rocks for weights. Joiners and coopers added to the din. In one corner did a potter form clay in the shape of a grand rooster for a model to be cast, then clapped round my featherless cock. And in another corner, keeping us all warm, was the forge where Max blissfully worked the bellows—while the smith himself beat fire-red iron into a grand framework worthy of Fortress Rosenberg's own clock.

I shook my head in wonder. These talents had lain fallow through the snows of winter. Now all within the castle worked with goodwill . . . always saving Lord Manfred himself and his retainers. Yet even some among them slipped into the workroom on occasion to follow our progress—or perhaps to assuage their boredom.

Thank you, Lord Jesus, for not making me a useless noble.

"Conrad?"

I turned. "Chris . . . tof. Ho! Has Cook changed you into a server?"

"We all do our part for the great clock of Rosenberg." She thrust a cup of ale at me from her tray. "To whet your whistle, Master Fool. Though the flour barrels scrape bottom, the ale still flows free." She lowered her voice to a whisper. "And serving brings back our old days together."

"But there is no braid for me to tug." I smiled.

"By the Virgin's grace, someday will it grow again."

"Christof!" the blacksmith roared. "My burning lungs need quenching!"

"By all the horned fiends!" Max yelled after him. "Mine, too!"

"See you give Max of the Second Chance a clip along

with his ale," I instructed Christa. "The forge is bringing out the worst in him."

"Aye." She grinned. "And it's a joy to hear!"

By the start of Holy Week, not only did my rooster have a coat of feathers painted over cast iron, but his wings flapped with each crow. Cook presided over him in her kitchen, unwilling to let the bird loose into Lord Manfred's claws.

"Mother Mary!" she prayerfully intoned over and over again. "What a marvel he'll be on Maundy Thursday during the telling of Gethsemane and the Stations of the Cross! Then will I set him upon the chapel's altar to crow for Saint Peter and us all!"

Unfortunately, progress was not so advanced on the great clock. True, its iron frame stood tall and proud—near twenty feet high!—and its columns were being enameled in bright hues of lapis blue as I watched. Its face was set within the high open circle, the twelve gilded signs of the zodiac adorning the Roman numerals of each hour. Two gilded hands radiating from the center waited to begin the telling of those hours. Yet in the cavernous space behind . . . nothing.

It was during our daily meetings in the kitchen after work was ended each day, after Lord Manfred's court had been fed on the castle's dwindling food reserves, that all were given their say. It was an openness suggested by me, and it was warming to see once silent, cowed servants find their voices. Yet I began to rue the liberty I'd bequeathed them. There were so many voices! Each added unplanned labor to the clock. Each suggestion delayed its completion— and brought the waiting sneers of guards Lucas and Nicholas too vividly close for comfort.

Joachim the Bellringer insisted each hour be rung with chimes. "For what good be a clock that cannot sing? What progress be that over my ringing of prime and vespers and compline?"

Alas, too true. I made note to discuss the problem with Oswald.

Next, the hours must be rung with *consecutive* bells, beginning with one and ending with twelve strikes. And then the figure striking the bell itself must be made symbolic. . . .

"It should take the form of an angel!" declared Cook.

"In Lord Manfred's domain?" protested Wilfred.

At which moment, old Father Lothair wandered absently through the kitchen. "Where have you hidden my altar wine, sinners? And if I'm to bless this clock of yours, none but Death may strike the hours. Such an undertaking requires an allegory for the brevity of life"—he stumbled over his robes and shakily righted himself—"a constant sermon, as it were. . . ."

"*Death* . . . ," sighed through the kitchen.

"Our lives be not hard enough," Cook muttered as she shoved a flagon of wine into the priest's hands and shooed him from her domain. "Now our beautiful clock must be marred with hideous skeleton and scythe—"

"Stay!" I made a sudden jingling flip of inspiration. "Death may have his day, but who's to say he can't be chased away?"

"Speak clearly, Conrad," Christa chided. "You are among friends."

Wagging my tongue at her, I spoke clearly. Soon the kitchen rang with laughter.

"A fine jest, indeed," Cook proclaimed, blessing my idea with a shake of her spoon.

Maundy Thursday the works were set into the case. The threat hanging over me of permanent residence within Manfred's dank dungeons began receding. I breathed more freely. Swaying on a ladder behind the frame, Oswald poked and prodded. "More grease upon this wheel, Master Carpenter."

Wilfred raced up with his pot of grease.

"Hell's bells," Max swore. "Will it never be ready for the testing?"

Oswald tottered down. "First it must be set in its final resting place, for the moving might jostle the works from out of their alignment."

I'd taken breath too soon. The next task was easier said than done. The clock's home was to be the great banqueting hall—at the opposite end from Manfred's dais. Thus might he gaze upon its glory to heart's content during his feasting. Every able-bodied man set shoulders and strength to the vast device. Cautiously was it laid upon the straw bed of the wheeled cart built for this very purpose. Slowly was it edged into the corridor and wheeled to the very entrance of the banqueting hall—

"Christ's wounds!"

The archway was not wide enough to admit the clock.

So did the crash of hammers and moans and groans of all give voice to Our Lord's Passion during the ritual Stations of the Cross in the neighboring chapel. So did they continue through the long night into Good Friday as the stonemasons made haste to rebuild the arch. As the noon bells dirged the very moment of Lord Jesus's death—only then did we set the clock in place at last.

"Ticktock," Grock pleaded, "start clock!"

But all the workmen backed away. Dropping their tools, they silently disappeared to do penance for their immortal souls.

"Holy thorns!" Max cried. "After all that sweat—"

This time Christa did give him a clip—a sharp one, too. The endless night had tried us all. "You should be doing penance for your tongue, Max, and your impatience, and—" She halted, close to tears.

I gathered both downcast boys to give my dove a moment's respite. "We finished too late. We must wait for Our Lord's resurrection on Easter morn. No one dare labor till then, lest he be accused of sacrilege."

"What *sac-ri* . . . ?" Grock tried for the word and failed.

"Not honoring Lord Jesus at this holiest feast of the year," I explained.

He stared at the clock. Thought very hard. Rubbed his stomach. "Grock hungry."

I shook my head. "The kitchen fires are dead. The whole castle must fast this day, Grock."

His face scrunched as his fists bunched. Next would come the deluge. "Grock *hungry!*"

I turned to Christa for saving. She swiped at her eyes, then knelt before the dwarf. "Lord Jesus is hungry, too. You may eat tomorrow, but *He* can't eat till Sunday morning. Come with me to the chapel." Rising, she took his hand. "You will see how hungry He looks upon the cross." She nodded at Max. "You, too, young sir. It will do your soul good to mourn for Our Lord."

He shrugged her off. "I've already done all me penance and mourning for a lifetime. It's the benefits of resurrection I'm still waiting on."

I looked from Max to the clock and back again. He'd spoken my deepest thoughts. Would the great clock of Rosenberg resurrect me and mine on Easter morn?

EIGHTEEN

This is the day which the Lord has made,
Let us exult and rejoice in it.
Alleluia, Alleluia, Alleluia!

Good Saint Francis always was ready for joy.
Now do I raise my voice with his: Alleluia!

The most high Mass of Easter Sunday was cele-
brated with pomp and circumstance. Lord Jesus
was risen from the dead! The new year was begun.
Alas, I was not privileged to partake in the sacred ceremony. Yet incense and prayers swirled around me where I
kept my own prayerful vigil over the great clock.

"*Ticktock,*" *sang the silent clock. "Time's folly will I watch.*"
Aye, and mine, too.

Would Oswald's final calibration of the works to my pre-
cise orders stand firm? Would it tick? Would it chime?
Would it—

"*Ite, missa est, alleluia, alleluia!*"

"*Deo gratias, alleluia, alleluia!*"

Father Lothair's final words and his congregation's joyful response signaled the end of the Mass. Signaled my release from endless fears. I rose from my knees. The moment of truth was at hand.

Lord Manfred of Rosenberg processed from the chapel into his banqueting hall with Lady Afra on his arm—and Precious the hawk on hers. His entire court followed in full plumage: the hems of their brilliant new robes and gowns sweeping over the freshly laid rushes of the floor, the fashionably curled toes of their shoes adding mincing movements to their stately steps. The promenade halted when Manfred did, midway in the long aisle between his dais and the clock. As if by clockwork, the retinue turned to view our wonder. Already anxiously attending it were the artisans who'd helped in its crafting, and Cook and her staff, who had miraculously found food in a hungry castle to keep these workers' stomachs full. All these cautiously lined the walls around the hall. As for me, I cockily perched upon a nearby table with Christa, Max, and Grock gathered close to hand. My brave show of confidence was a sham.

My very life now depended upon the the great clock of Rosenberg.

Into the hush of suspense filling the space—near echoing from the very rafters—I deliberately jingled my ass's ears. His lordship took note of the challenge.

"Fool!" Manfred ordered. "Start my clock!"

I glanced at the hourglass Max passionately clutched beside me. The sands had nearly run their course. The timing should be perfect, if Oswald's calibrations had been correct. If . . . if . . . if . . .

Leaping from perch into flip, I cartwheeled through the crowd to the very base of the clock. Springing to my feet, I hugged the enameled frame with a prayer that it harbored more than mere gloss. Then I reached for the immense hanging pendulum with another prayer. This for my preservation. Finally, I swung the pendulum into its swaying motion. . . .

A tremendous groaning of wheels and gears commenced, after which came—

Thank you, Lord Jesus!

—a steady *ticktock, ticktock.*

Emboldened by the imposing tones, I faced Lord Manfred and his court. Made a fine bow.

"At your command, this work began. Now do the craftsmen with me make gift to thee . . . of the finest clock in history! As Christ rose on this Easter morn, so rises a clock that none may scorn." I caught Max's eyes across the hall. He nodded frantically. "Only watch and listen—as the noon bell's chime doth lead us to Heaven!"

I sprang away to watch the huge face with the others— the huge face with both hands deliberately set to but a fraction before twelve. In the midst of the ponderous ticking did hour hand and minute hand meet.

Click.

A pause—infinitely long to my racing heart—before a portal beneath the great clock's face slid open.

"*Ahhhh . . .*" swept through the hall.

Gliding into view came Death himself, his skull grimacing mightily as he swung scythe against bell.

The first peal rang out.

Amid the court's gasp, Death was jostled forward by a mighty falcon—talons spread wide to grasp the Grim Reaper.

The second peal tolled.

"The Rosenberg honor!" Manfred exclaimed.

But there was more. At each new strike, figures from my workshop danced in mad pursuit: Wilfred with his saw, Master Cooper with a barrel stave, the burly smith with hammer in hand, Oswald the Alchemist bearing vile-looking beakers. Near everyone had been included. The eighth image was humpbacked Grock, with his rocking gait and bunched fists. The ninth was Max with bellows. . . . I smiled at the tenth: a golden, winged Christa. The eleventh figure? Conrad the Good, in cap and bells, careening along in a cartwheel. But the best was saved for last—for here came Cook herself, her great swinging wooden spoon the most lethal weapon of all. I grinned. If anyone could catch Lord Death and give him a good beating, it was Cook.

I'd hardly heard the cries of surprise and admiration that heralded each new figure, each consecutive strike of Death's scythe on his bell. But as the statue of Cook seemed to put on a burst of speed in her frenzied chase, as the figures disappeared and the door below the clock's face swung shut with finality—then did I hear the overwhelming silence.

Every head turned toward Manfred. A vast communal breath was taken . . . and held. Soon the ladies would begin to swoon. . . .

Lord Manfred of Rosenberg raised his arms, shook the wide sleeves of his robe, and began to clap. Slowly. Majestically. I was magnetized by the gesture and what it showed.

He'd gilded his talons for the sacred day!

Barely did my shudder pass than his court followed suit with dignified applause. Surrounding us all, the castle's staff cheered and hooted with abandon. They'd like to have continued till the clock's midnight display twelve hours hence, but Manfred raised his arms again. Silence returned. Now he directed his attention to me.

"You have done well, Master Fool. You may approach."

No flips or handstands or cartwheels. I strode to him like a man. Bowed respectfully.

"My lord."

"I would reward you for this worthy service."

He reached into his robe for his purse and tossed it to me. I felt the weight of gold briefly. Very briefly. Then like a catapult did I lob it across the breadth of the hall—to Cook, who dropped her spoon in amazement as it fell into her hands.

A nod to Manfred. "My thanks, but the gold be for your castle family. Never has such served so faithfully."

A flicker of anger, covered by a wry shrug of acceptance. "And for you, Conrad the Good?"

Another bow. "For me and *my* family, no gold is due. Instead, three boons I would pursue."

His talons twitched as his eyes went between the clock and me. He was shrewd enough to know that I had given him a princely gift. What other lord within the entire empire of Germany was master of his own clock? As I watched, I could see him toting up these thoughts in his head, as if on an abacus. Could see his prestige, his political future, expanding endlessly in his brain.

"Speak."

Much had I pondered during my long vigil. If success was mine, what reward would I seek? What does a fool need? What does *this* fool need?

"Three things only do I ask: a goodly horse with goodly tack—"

"Done."

He did not deign to hesitate. One of his many horses was an insignificance. I plowed forward.

"Next I do request to take your dwarf from out his nest—"

"Grock?" Manfred was incredulous. "You would waste your boon on a driveling idiot?"

I merely smiled and watched him turn to his wife. Lady Afra sniffed disdain through her long nose and caressed her hawk's feathers. "I have long since grown weary of the creature."

"He is yours," his lordship proclaimed. "And last?"

There was not air enough in Lord Manfred's fortress domain to ease my lungs, my pounding heart, for what I would ask next. Yet I rallied all within me and caught those hooded eyes.

"Lastly, I appeal you decree upon us freedom, with a seal"—I turned to Christa and Max and Grock, hovering protectively nearby—"that we may wander through the land beholden to no earthly man."

This *did* set his veins to throbbing.

Ticktock . . . ticktock . . . ticktock.

My great clock counted the seconds, then minutes, as Lord Manfred of Rosenberg struggled with the hateful word. *Freedom.* In planning for this moment, I had struggled with the word myself. But there was no other that would do. Nothing but an official declaration of our status as *free men* would save us from being forced into service by any petty lordling we met. *Any* lordling—like Manfred himself, who had immediately presumed upon his power to imprison me with his demands.

The entire hall jumped as the half hour struck.

Manfred collected himself. "It shall be done. Yet see you do vacate my fiefdom ere I look upon you again!"

My last bow hid my triumph. "Your will is my command!"

"Let the feasting begin!" ringing in my ears, I wrested my little band from Lord Manfred of Rosenberg's claws at last.

NINETEEN

Rise up, my love, my fair one, and come away.

For, lo, the winter is past, the rain is over and gone;

The flowers appear on the earth; the time of the singing of birds is come, and the voice of the turtle is heard in our land.

Without my notice, the spring thaw had begun. Like unto Solomon, I felt my heart rise with the re-born land.

"Here now, what kind of shoddy work you trying to foist off on us?" Max, in full dudgeon, displayed the left forehoof of our boon horse to the waiting farrier. "Hell's bells! The iron in this shoe's so thin it won't see us off your perishing mountain!" He glared up. "Seems to me his lordship give us a 'goodly horse, with goodly tack.'"

The farrier paled. "Rest assured, Master Max. All will be put in order. A complete new set of shoes for Brandy, and Master Conrad's mount as well . . ."

Swallowing a snicker, I left our new gelding in Max's capable hands. He was a strong young bay with a distinctive flagon-like marking on his forehead, and I'd chosen him purposely to be Blackspur's companion—without fear of competition. I hated to even think what grief another stallion might portend. And a mare would be equally distracting. By Saint Francis, I would have peace and harmony among my traveling comrades, human and animal alike.

Wandering to the far end of the stables, I found the saddler completing my other requests. "How goes it, Kurt?"

He pulled a needle from his mouth. "Give me but another day, Conrad. Never have I been asked to make *double* saddles. Two of them!"

"You've added the special backrest for Christof?"

"Aye."

"And taken special pains for Grock?"

"Aye." He motioned to the formed leather he was working. "Measured his seat, I did, and gave him a little extra support to the front and rear. And he'll be having an extra-high pommel for his short arms to hang on to."

I bent to admire his labor. "You do fine work, Master Kurt."

He beamed and leaned back over his stitching. Abandoning him to it, I ran the other preparations through my mind: sufficient saddlebags for provisions, extra garments, bedding. . . . I walked absently through the outer ward.

"Why the frown, Sir Fool?"

I spun. "Sparrow!"

"Hush. The court begins to take the air."

She made for the parapet steps and I followed, admiring the lithe, boyish stride she'd perfected so well. Above the inner curtain, we leaned against the wall. Stared at the rivulets of snowmelt racing down into the valley. I sighed.

"It feels like a caravan I'm preparing, not two horses!"

"Was freedom so much easier when there was but you and Blackspur for the leaving?"

"Aye," I admitted. "But then there was a stray bird that could not be left fluttering around Otto's moat. . . ."

Christa smiled. "And Max hanging by his neck from the gallows tree, waiting for his second chance."

"Now Grock," I finished, "who, left behind, would be dead from disfavor before the seasons change again."

She reached for my hand. "Is it so terrible, then, having a family?"

A hawk Manfred had not yet managed to capture and enchain swept over my head. I followed its sharp flight. Across the valley. To the far mountains. Beyond. Then did I smile.

"Nay. Our flight will be slower, but richer. There is time for our questing, wiser questing. Much time." I brought her fingers to my lips. "Will you still come away with me, my love?"

She caressed my cheek. "Silly Conrad!"

✳ ✳ ✳

"Grock Conrad's boy! Grock Conrad's boy!"

The truth had dawned upon the dwarf when I set him on Brandy's back in his special seat in front of Max.

"Max Grock's brother! Max Grock's brother!"

To his delirious chanting, I surveyed our little caravan, then pulled myself astride Blackspur. I groped for Christa's hands, felt their warm pressure, and nudged my horse toward the gatehouse.

Thus, on April Fools' Day, we escaped Manfred of Rosenberg's gray fortress at last. Half the castle bid us farewell from atop the outer curtain's walls. But it was Cook's great wooden spoon as it swung over us like a pendulum, anointing us with blessings, that I will remember always.

"Set your mind to the path, Conrad." Christa's arms tightened around me. "It looks muddy and treacherous and—"

I caught the catch in her voice. "Do you weep for them?"

"I weep for all good friends we'll ne'er see again."

"Blackspur!" I cleared my throat lest I choke on my own sorrow. "Blackspur! Mind your Brother Sheep that this way come. They were not blessed with your intelligence!"

Blackspur tossed his great neck and nimbly stepped between the flock of spring lambs being herded up the slope to refill the castle's larders. Behind us, Grock changed his tune to *baa* with glee.

"Stop bouncing, squirt!" Max groused from behind him. "Lord Christ! You want us tumbling off the mountain's side?"

Christa and I burst into laughter. And so we slipped and slid from Manfred's aerie. The mud was thicker still in the lowlands of the valley, but our mounts high-stepped past mired carts and swearing peasants.

"Good day to you, sirs!" we cried. And, "God be with you!" Then on we pranced through the town of Kronach, east into the wilds of the Frankenwald beyond.

"Another blessed mountain!" Max complained. "Where are we going?"

"Away!" I gaily answered.

And it was so.

Could ever a moment be riper? *Never.*

Thus did I take special pains for our resting place that night. It must be in a glade, beneath towering trees—trees worthy to form the arches of our own cathedral. Brother Sun gifted his last warm smiles to us as I reined in Blackspur.

"What think you, sparrow?"

Christa eased against her backrest, the better to study the noble spruce, the rays of falling light, the soft carpet of needles awaiting us. "It is lovely!"

"Lovely enough to be our wedding bower?"

"Conrad! *Oh, Conrad* . . ."

And then she was truly weeping.

"Princess!" Grock yelped. "Conrad hurt you?"

"No! He has made me happy. So happy—"

"Why cry?" Grock insisted.

"Peace!" I leaped from Blackspur's back. "It's past time for Grock and Max to make themselves useful to this family enterprise."

"Blow horn?" Grock asked.

"Yes! There will be a great blowing of horns and a great rattling of tambourines. For tonight do Christa and I wed!"

"Faith!" Max spit out. "And about time!"

I held my tongue till I swung both boys off their mount. Then I eyed young Max. "If you don't want the thrashing of your very life, go and teach Grock how to collect wood. *Huge* quantities of wood for our nuptial fire!"

"God's truth! I meant no insult—"

I gifted the lad with a ferocious scowl. "Repent by your labors."

As Max dragged Grock off, I reached up for my dove. "Alone at last!"

She laughed within my arms. "I fear we will never truly be alone again."

"Then we must learn to live for the rare intervals of reprieve." I availed myself of our reprieve and her lips.

As night enveloped us, I knelt before Grock. "This is the most important playing of your life. Do you understand?"

He gripped his horn with fervor. "Aye, Conrad."

I quickly glanced around. All was in readiness. A fire burned brightly in the center of our nuptial grove. Blackspur and Brandy were companionably hobbled to one side. Near the horses, Max's and Grock's blankets lay waiting under the sheltering boughs of a tree . . . while on the far side of the clearing rose our *wedding tent*. Its magnificence brought a joyous smile. I'd been right to take Cook into my confidence on the subject. . . .

"Fie! And the truth before my eyes all this time! Mistress Seamstress and her helpers will stitch a tent for you lovebirds worthy of his lordship's campaigns! Greased against the weather, with more fringe than all the Turks of the Holy Land!"

"Yet small," I'd begged. "It must be carried on Blackspur's back. And *intimate*—"

"You sly fox, you!" Cook's ham of a hand had slammed the breath from me.

Even now I blushed in remembrance.

"Time, Conrad?" Grock asked.

I stood up and pulled off my fool's cap. "Aye, Sir Herald. Blow your horn!"

Ta-da! Ta-da! Ta-da!

"Hear ye, hear ye! To Sister Moon and Heaven above, I do announce the sacred banns of marriage between Conrad the Good and Christa the Fair!" I flung my head back toward the patch of stars. "Be there any Above or Below who would dispute the excellence of this union, speak now—or forever hold your peace!"

The night's silence descended on our glade. I paused to revel in its sweetness before again signaling Grock.

Ta-da! Ta-da! Ta-da!

I took a deep breath. "Who now will give Christa the Fair into my hands?"

The tent's flap spread open. Out crawled Max. He made a fuss about straightening his tunic, then reached back inside for Christa's arm. Out she flowed—

"*Holy Mary, Mother of us all!*" I whispered.

"Princess!" Grock prayed in awe.

For here was Christa unbound, in a gown worthy of a noble lady. Max gave us a long moment for admiration before he possessively tucked her arm in his and slowly marched her across the clearing to me.

"Here's your prince then, Angel. . . ." He faltered and began again. "Never seen the likes of the both of you. If God Himself don't bless you, I'll be after Him with me hammer. Just see if I don't!"

"Thank you, Max of the Second Chance." I reached for Christa's hands before he got himself in deeper trouble with the Almighty. Then I looked into my beloved's eyes. They flashed with the firelight but would have held heat enough without.

"Christa . . . dearest Christa. Before God and man, I do take thee for my wife. As long as laughter grows, as long as breath still flows . . . through Earth to Heaven I will follow thee. With bells of joy will I enfold you in my music and my love. More I cannot say. . . . Will you have me?"

My beloved lowered her eyes, then raised them again. Now did they burn with pride and love—so fiercely, I near backed away from the flames.

"My Good Conrad, with heart and soul will I have thee. With all my being do I take thee for my husband . . . through this life to Heaven beyond."

I sighed and drew her into my arms. Under Nature's cathedral, we sealed our vows with a holy kiss.

Ta-da, ta-da, ta-da!

Rat-a-tat-a-rat-a-tat-a-tat!

Max and Grock danced around our embrace with tambourine and horn.

"The wedding feast!" Max cried.

"Food!" Grock yelled.

Never did toasted bread and cheese taste so ambrosial. Never was wine as honeyed as the flagon of Lord Manfred's finest that Cook had slipped us. I confess we took the precaution of sharing its richness too profligately with Max and Grock. I smiled as their heads began nodding clear down to their chins.

"A wise woman, Cook." I turned to Christa and her finery. "I see you took her into your confidence as well."

My sparrow laughed. "Set those two in their beds. Then may you escort me to our nuptial tent so the gown and wine may be used to best advantage!"

I did my beloved's bidding . . . and better advantage was never taken.

TWENTY

May good Saint Wolfgang, good Saint Peter
(whose key can Heav'n unlock)
Throat of wolf and vixen block,
Blood from shedding, bone from crunching!
Help me, the holy one,
Who ill hath never done,
And his holy wounds
Keep my herd from all wood-hounds!

Dante's tales of Hell are harrowing, yet but one
man's fancy. How to explain—and address—the
strangenesses of our own Middle Earth? I was not
too proud to fall upon a simple herdsman's charm
in defense of my own herd.

With the sheer abandon of love, I led my little family willy-nilly through the mountain wilds. There was no destination but the first wildflowers to weave into a crown for my princess's head, or the sight of doe and fawns bounding through the forest, or mother boar snuffling along with bristly piglets in tow. Early did we retire to bed, late did we arise. Often did we pause for Max and Grock to run free while my sparrow and I relished more moments alone. Then did we pause again so I might school Blackspur in the tricks his long winter rest had near stolen from his memory. My family enjoyed this schooling as much as my horse.

"Only see what a mighty charger is Blackspur!" I declared from astride his back.

In an open meadow, with Brandy closely watching—in hopes, I am certain, that his turn be next—I worked through the movements my father had first described to me from his youth spent watching tourneys in a rich elector's household.

"The great tournaments of jousting are but practice for skill at arms," I explained. "Horse and rider must be one to ride against the charging lances of the enemy—as Blackspur and I have always been one." I bent to whisper in his ear. *"Turn."*

Prompted by pressure from my thighs, my horse leaned back on his haunches and made a full circling turn.

"More!" Grock yelled.

So Blackspur and I did repeat the turn till I was satisfied it was perfected, satisfied he had accomplished it within the tightest area possible for his huge frame.

"And next," I announced, "trotting in place!"

It was an exercise more difficult than it appeared, since the cadence must be perfect, the legs nobly elevated—

"Hell's bells," Max complained. "How's that going to help in a battle?"

"Must everything be about warfare?" Christa asked. "This is like watching a poem!"

"Yet not showy enough." I stilled Blackspur and patted his neck. "Well done, my friend, but we must give young Max the rear charge you used under his hanging tree."

As I put my hands, arms, and legs into full use, Blackspur took a prodigious leap forward. Half rearing, he drew his hocks under and made another jump forward, kicked out his hind legs viciously . . . then landed solidly on all four feet.

"*Holy Lord.*" Max was impressed at last. "Could do some damage with that, he could!"

I smiled. "For enemies from the rear. For enemies to the front—"

So did I set my powerful Blackspur back on his haunches, freeing his forelegs for a frontal attack. Max and Christa cheered. Grock cried, "More!"

"Another day." I flipped back to earth to cosset my horse. "Blackspur has remembered his lessons well enough for this one."

Max took being a big brother seriously. When Christa praised him for his care of Grock as our horses ambled side by side along an overgrown track the next day, he scowled.

"Never had one before, have I? Can't count the three

what expired before the midwife even cut their cords. God's truth, it's only the last I remember. Bluish, he was. And Mutter's wail—"

At my sparrow's gasp, I reined in Blackspur. "Here's a fine meadow with greening grass for Blackspur and Brandy to graze themselves fat upon." I turned to its border. "And woods with budding leaves for Max and Grock to explore while Christa and I ready provisions for *our* stomachs!"

So it was that as we finished dining on hard sausage and dried apples, Max decided to teach Grock the mysteries of tree climbing. Stretched lazily upon our blanket table, I grinned, watching him talk the dwarf up a low-hanging bow nearby. There Grock clutched, slipped, and hung dangling upside down, deciding whether or not to be frightened. Whether or not to cry. Christa finally took note with a sigh of exasperation.

"Praise cometh before a fall. In Heaven's name, Max, have pity on Grock. He's like to break his head!"

"Don't fuss, sparrow. It's only a few lengths, and he has need to learn confidence."

Grock twisted, and his expression changed. "Holy tree! Conrad see!"

With a shrug of inevitability, I cast off sloth and rose. "What is it?"

"Hell's bells!" Max yelled. "The squirt's right!"

Christa joined us while I rescued Grock and set him upon his feet. As the blood in his reddened face settled, he pointed up at the tree's bark. "Holy!"

"Someone's carved crosses in the trunk," Christa said. "Three of them!"

"Here's another lot on this tree." Max began prowling deeper into the woods. We followed. "And another . . ."

In the meadow behind us, Blackspur neighed. I ignored him to inspect Max's finds. "The pattern is the same . . . three crosses with a space between them, set within a triangle—"

" 'Tis for the Wood-Wives' sanctuary, when the Devil be after hunting them."

We all four whirled at the voice, grating as if out of use. It came from the first soul we'd met since taking to the mountains. Shaggy, he was, with wildly matted hair and unkempt beard. Rough sheepskins covered his body like to John the Baptist in the wilderness, while one gnarled hand grasped a staff taller than himself.

I recovered first. "God keep you, Master Shepherd. You came upon us unexpected."

"Aye." Civilities complete, he struck his rod at the ground—so hard the earth did seem to shake. "What be ye doing intruding upon the forbidden woods?"

"Only . . . passing through."

He glared through milky eyes. "Make haste to see ye pass beyond. This be Wotan's realm." Another thrust of his staff, and its intricate carvings winked as they caught an errant ray of sunlight. "The moon wanes, the juices drain, his wood-hounds build their thirst for blood!"

Christa quickly crossed herself, and when I looked back, the old man was gone.

"*Christ Lord!*" Max exclaimed. "What was that about?"

Grock only gaped open-jawed, the first signs of dribble in weeks marring his chin.

"Ho!" I made to shake my bells, then remembered I hadn't worn them since our wedding night. "My father, Hans the Large—" I scooped up Grock and gave him a tickle. "Did I ever tell you of my wonderful father, Hans the Large?" He giggled and his jaw shut. "Well did he know all the old forest tales. Of moss-women; and old Baumesel, the Ass of the Trees; and Wotan himself, god of the forests."

And leader of the Wild Hunt and carrier-off of the dead.

But these things I did not say. I loped toward our blanket and the waiting horses. "Were my father here, he would have you laughing well. But as the day wanes with the moon, I think we will travel on."

In short shrift did I have my family mounted and away.

"Conrad?" Max's voice was very small next to Christa and me as he clutched Brandy's reins in a white-knuckled grip. "That old shepherd. He looked mossy green. And where were his sheep?"

Both points had I duly noted. Blackspur's warning, too. I reached for one of Christa's arms as she silently hugged me. "He looked hungry enough to have eaten them. I did intend to invite him to dine. . . . But look! Here is another meadow! With sheep upon it!"

"Cock's soul!" Max recovered his native belligerence

fast. "Do you grow as old as Oswald and need spectacles? Those be deer!"

"Conrad *not* old!" Grock yelled.

"How can a baby like you tell?" Max shot back.

"Grock *not* baby! Grock have many birth days!"

"How many?"

Then Grock began to count in his own way. "Manfred buy me . . . for lady gift. Ask village how old. Village say, 'Grock live with pigs . . . this long.'"

My diversionary tactic had succeeded beyond my wildest expectations. Not only had Grock produced practically an entire paragraph of speech, but he'd begun to answer questions I'd thought unanswerable. I turned to watch him hold up ten stubby fingers, then another five.

"Lord Jesus save us!" Max ignored his *little* brother's superior age completely. "You lived with *pigs*?"

"Much food," Grock declared. "Manfred food better. Princess food best."

Christa sighed into my ear as I set Blackspur to a trot. So did Grock's age increase till he surpassed my own. So did I distance my loved ones from the mysteries of the pagan god Wotan's forbidden forest. Such things—in company with my wolves—cannot be forgotten but are best buried in silence.

I took the precaution of setting up camp in a meadow that night. Yet it was a small meadow, surrounded by woods. Dark woods. What else could one expect upon a night mountain? Barely had Christa and I retired to our wedding tent than I heard the hesitant shuffle of feet outside the flap. I waited beneath our lambskin.

"Conrad?" Max's voice was small again.

"Have you and Grock said your prayers?"

"Aye, but I think it will rain—"

"Rain!" Grock echoed.

"The sky was clear when last I looked upon it."

"*Raaa-in!*" Grock wailed. "Get wet. Sick. *Die.*"

Christa twisted from my arms—

"Only this night, dear Conrad."

—and spread wide the flap.

So did our intimate tent become hopelessly intimate. I lay awake long after Max and Grock contentedly burrowed between my sparrow and me. Listening to their sleep. Listening for Wotan's wood-hounds in mad pursuit of their prey across the skies.

Every catastrophe that Wotan presaged having filled my dreams, by morning I determined it was time our idyll ended. Time our quest be renewed. So did I resolutely point Blackspur in a new direction. South. Alas, escaping the mountain wilds was far harder than entering them. Several hours of traveling in what I took to be a southerly, *descending* direction brought us not to an open valley but—

"*Christ's foe!*" Max yelped. "What d'you call *that?*"

I shrugged helplessly. "I don't know. I'm just a poor fool, remember?"

Spread out before us was an incredible landscape.

"Rocks!" Grock yelled. "*Big* rocks!"

"*Boulders,*" Christa clarified. "Big rocks are called *boulders.*"

Rocks, boulders . . . the drop before us revealed a hilly labyrinth of them. *Enormous* boulders they were: round and majestic in royal isolation, piled atop each other, fallen, sprouting great pines, cascading like stone fountains . . . as far as the eye could see. I turned to Christa.

"What think you? Should we go back?"

She studied the forest from which we'd emerged. Shivered. "I've seen enough of this mountain, Conrad."

Only too well did I understand. I nudged Blackspur down into the labyrinth.

Vague premonitions having troubled me all the morn, this time when Blackspur neighed, I took heed.

We'd been tentatively working our way single file between boulders and their lengthening shadows for near an hour when he trumpeted his warning.

"Stay back!" I hissed to Max behind. To Christa, I murmured, "Hold for your very life!"

Only just in time.

Out of the shadows ahead sprang armed men in torn and rusting chain mail—one . . . two . . . *three* of them, blocking our passage with upraised swords.

"*Halt!* Your horses or your lives!"

Good Saint Wolfgang keep us. Soldiers from old wars still lost in the land. Other hounds I had not thought upon. They'd be craving more than our horses. The closest mercenary proved me right. Staring past me at Christa, his thick lips twisted into a leer.

"That one be fair enough for use. I claims him!"

"Nay, Hellhound!" All qualms gone, I bent toward Blackspur's head.

"*Front attack!*"

Then did my horse and I become one again. Arms and knees guiding his great bulk, so did he rear, so did he place his weight upon his haunches . . . so did his powerful forefeet lash out. I had no need to name the enemy. Blackspur owned more than mere instinct.

"*Ai-eeeeeeeeeee!*"

The first cur fell.

Another swung his sword. Blackspur avoided the slashing blade with his next rear. His ironclad hooves found their mark.

A gasp of disbelief, then, "Lord Satan's . . . *caught me at last!*"

The second fell.

Heaving for breath, I readied Blackspur for the third attack—

"Stay!" Steel clanged against stone as the third blackguard dropped his sword and cowered against the nearest boulder. "Quarters! I cry for quarter! Keep the Devil Horse away!"

"Mercy? You dare beg for mercy when none would have been shown to me and mine?" My blood boiled hot . . . yet he *had* surrendered. I tossed my head, then dropped my horse to all four feet, nudging him headfirst into the cringing fellow. It was gratifying to see Blackspur snort and bare his teeth at the scurvy knave. Gratifying to watch the blood drain from the filthy, scarred face.

I leaned over Blackspur's neck. Stared into crazed eyes. "Are there more of you?"

"Nay, nay! We three mercenaries alone, cast out by our Free Company."

"Why are you in this place?"

His grunt was incredulous. "To hide—and swoop down upon the town but an hour's distance beyond."

It was sufficient intelligence. "Max!" I ordered. "Come forward."

From behind another stone giant, Max came upon Brandy, Grock with his hands still plastered tightly over his eyes in terror.

"Dismount and bind this despicable rogue with his belt."

"God's truth! It'll be me pure pleasure, Conrad!"

"Wait! Mind the other two, should they come to their senses."

Max leaped to earth with remarkable enthusiasm. I watched as he gave each body a vigorous boot. "No fear here, Conrad," he reported with satisfaction. "Blackspur's kicked them straight to Hell."

My sparrow shuddered back to life behind me. Max took

note. His eyes hardened. "An it were up to me, I'd not be binding this last one but finishing off the poxy bastard with his own sword. Wasn't it a Free Company of raiders as swept into my village? Didn't they put the lot to the sword—after having their way with every woman, girl, and babe in sight? Didn't they sack and burn every house clear down to the ground?" His face crumpled, and with it his righteous anger. "Me fader's smithy, too," followed in a whisper. "And him within it—"

Vaulting from Blackspur's back, I caught Max to me. Hugged hard. He shook like one with the palsy.

"An' me like a . . . c-coward," Max whimpered. "Up to me neck in the . . . *privy hole* . . . where Fader tossed me for safekeeping—"

"Conrad!" Grock screamed. *"Knife!"*

Loosing Max, I spun. Dagger in hand, our prisoner was breaking away from Blackspur, *making toward my Christa.* The heart within me stopped . . . yet before I could breathe, move, Blackspur made a half turn on his haunches and lunged into a rear charge. His deadly hooves struck. Again. And again. Then before my disbelieving eyes did my horse turn yet again—to attack the villainous churl with his forefeet, and pursue his attack till my gorge did rise.

"Blackspur, enough. Stop!"

I dragged our magnificent defender from the battered pulp of the cutthroat. "Mighty warrior!" I laid my head against his. "Peerless friend!" The battle lust in his eyes dimmed.

When the heaving beneath his foam-flecked skin subsided at last, I turned my face up to Christa.

"You held on."

"*Holy Mary, Mother of God, pray for us sinners. . . .*" She swayed off Blackspur into my arms.

And there I stood within those imprisoning walls of stone . . . cradling my beloved, head swinging between Death and the rest of my shattered family.

Good Lord Jesus, guide me like a wise rider. Be one with me.

"Max!" I barked at last to the lad, sprawled in dust and mourning. "Collect the weapons. They will make a fine gift to the mayor of the beleaguered town beyond. Grock! Ready yourself. For you will be the bearer of this fine gift!"

Only then was I ready to kiss my dove back to life. Her eyes slowly opened.

"Is it finished?"

"Aye."

"May we return to human society?"

"Clever wench." I rewarded her with another kiss. "You guessed my brilliant plan."

TWENTY-ONE

O Fortune,
like the moon
you are changeable,
ever waxing
and waning;
hateful life
first oppresses
and then soothes
as fancy takes it;
poverty
and power
it melts them like ice.

Fortune's wheel spins on. . . .

"I would speak to your mayor!"
　　We limped into the town beyond the labyrinth, dusty, battle-weary, and bearing arms—a contingent

that included a warhorse, a dwarf, and a wild-haired lad sporting a gilded neckband. Small wonder the few residents we met scattered like harried rabbits. I halted our horses in the center of the square and raised my voice.

"In God's name would I speak to your headman! We bring news of succor from your travails!"

From my lofty perch, I surveyed the collection of half-timbered buildings surrounding the church. One door cautiously opened. A balding head poked out.

"Who seeks the mayor of Alexandersbad?"

I squared my shoulders. "Conrad the Good. Freeman, jester to nobility, and—with my comrades—destroyer of the mercenaries lately raiding your defenseless town."

"You have proof?"

I sighed and reached into my pouch. "Proof of free status here." I waved Manfred's rolled document, with its impressive scarlet wax seal. Jammed my fool's cap upon my head and shook its ears. "Proof of calling with these bells." Pointed toward Grock's heavy load. "And proof of our deed with these captured weapons, which we freely give into your hands." A pause. "Should you wish to accept them."

The mayor thought hard, then took the bold step of leaving the safety of his doorway.

"Hell's bells!" Max fumed. "What does it take to—"

"*Hush!*" Christa warned.

The hesitant man halted at a safe distance. "How many did you defeat?"

"Three."

"No more? We thought sure from the viciousness of their night incursions that they be a score or more—"

"Only *three*."

Of a sudden, the square was alive with people. It was unnecessary to formally present the swords. A crushing swarm snatched them from Grock's lap with bloodthirsty howls. I near cringed in fear they'd be turned against *us*, the town's defenders. Yet, in the end, were we received like conquering heroes. Snatched off Blackspur and Brandy as precipitously as the weapons, so were we raised upon shoulders and jolted about the square as our horses were led off, hopefully to their much-deserved rewards. The church bells clanged till the square was filled with every man, woman, child, and mangy dog of Alexandersbad. While a delegation of the heartiest burghers—well armed with our swords—set off to verify the absolute obliteration of their town's scourge, our tale must be told again. And yet again—

"Nay," I protested at last. "My throat grows dry!"

"Merciful God!" the cry rose. "Is this the thanks we give our saviors?"

Then were tables pulled from the inn, barrels rolled out, and Alexandersbad began to celebrate in earnest. I had no cause for complaint, nor did my family, isolated at our benched table like an island within the surging waters of touching, blessing folk. Goodly ale was offered, and wine. Next came rich stew and fresh bread, hot from the oven, till finally an entire suckling pig was laid before us. Grock opened his mouth wide enough to be stuffed with the apple in the pig's maw.

Max's ale-glazed eyes sharpened. "Here now, this be more like it!" From deep within his tunic, he drew forth a dagger. The dagger last seen threatening my Christa.

I caught his arm. "Max—"

He yanked it free. Gave me a cold-blooded glare. "I *earned* this."

"So you did."

I backed off as he attacked the pig with relish. Its crisp skin and juicy flesh no longer beckoned me.

With dusk came the return of the burghers. They had done what we had not: stripped the bandits of everything—including heads and certain private body parts. Thrust upon spikes, these mementos were paraded through the square, accompanied by drummers and brightly burning torches. The mob grew savage with drink and the vengeance so long denied them. It troubled me greatly to have released such barbarous spirits—spirits as dark as any woodland menace. As the scarred face of our final tormentor leered past me, I gave thanks that Max and Grock already had their heads pillowed in sleep upon the boards, all innocence once more. Thanks that they would not have this new nightmare added to their own scarred lives. I leaned toward my pale and trembling sparrow.

"Escape, by the Holy Rood!" I implored. "Guest of honor or no, I cannot stomach more!"

"Nor I!" Christa spared a final look at the severed heads now bobbing and weaving around a growing bonfire. "The townsfolk forget us in their bloodlust. Only give me a moment." Beneath the boards, she pressed my hand for courage, then rose to catch the passing innkeeper. "Good host!" A brilliant smile. "Ten thousand thanks for your hospitality, but I fear weariness o'ertakes us. Have you a room where we may rest?"

He set down his tray. "Am I not the innkeeper? But follow me and you shall have my finest—as my personal guests!"

I hoisted Grock across a shoulder while Christa prodded Max into a shambling sleepwalk. Together we threaded through the crowd to the innkeeper's finest chamber. Finding the sole bed already well filled with lice, we huddled together on the roughly boarded floor. Still could I enfold my beloved within my arms. She shivered in my embrace.

"This was a day I would not wish to live again."

Raucous shouts, boisterous singing, and the sound of fisticuffs pursued us through the single open window. I held her tighter. "Yet we *live*."

Before dawn, I slipped from the inn, past sodden and snoring revelers littering the square, to the town stables. When the horses were readied, I fetched my family. We left Alexandersbad—dark in sight and dark in spirit—as stealthily as bandits, heading south as the sun rose.

I felt Christa twist behind me. Turned to watch her study where we'd been.

"It's gone from sight," she murmured at last. Then did she begin a Te Deum. As Blackspur pricked up his ears, I reached for my pipe to join the song of thanksgiving. Soon the *rat-a-tat-a-tat* of Max's tambourine joined us. Last came Grock's *ta-da, ta-da, ta-da!*

Blackspur and Brandy bolted in unison.

"Steady!"

Max and I reined back our horses to a trot.

"This is the *new* day the Lord has made," I proclaimed. "Alleluia!"

In the next weeks, we wandered south, always south—south toward the warmth of summer, south toward the hope of an enlightened master. We journeyed through valleys and onto plains filled with peasants at the plow and harrow, and on into villages and towns. If we liked the looks of these, we paused to give a show for our dinners. If not—if the punishment stocks be overfilled . . . if the poor sot caged in the village pillory be pelted too viciously with garbage . . . if the town gibbet be hung with fresh fruit—we moved on. Then had we to slowly and carefully spend my purse of coins for provisions. When coins became rare, one by one we began to barter Grock's string of pearls. There was money enough for us to live, love enough for us to thrive. I prayed it was not my imagining that slowly more and more of the stocks lay empty; more hanging trees lay bare of all but fresh leaves and nesting birds. They were goodly signs, and I took heart. These peaceful Bavarian fiefs must have a good master, indeed. Might not the next bend in the road, the top of the next hill, present the grail for which I quested?

In the meantime, thinking Blackspur already schooled well beyond our present needs, I began schooling my little troupe instead. Selecting a piece of meadow, or the edge of some peasant's field, I would set them through their paces—often collecting the odd shepherd or farmer to gape and clap at their free show. Soon they could succeed in more than just building a pyramid. So did we bloom with the springtime, acquiring the confidence of seasoned performers.

Following the gentle waters of the Isar River well into May, we were brought to the goodly town—nay, near city—of Landshut, much praised by folk along our way. I studied the fortress dominating its hill. Its roofs were red-tiled, its walls built of pleasing soft yellow stones and brick. It was imposing, yes, but had not the chill of Fortress Rosenberg. Instead, under the mantle of pure blue sky, it smiled like a protective father over the town below. Smiling with it, I nudged Blackspur, and we ambled through the city gates. Surely it was market day, for women were carrying empty baskets toward the center of town. I shook my bells and half bowed toward one.

"God be with you, Goodwife. We have traveled far to reach your excellent town. Can you name me the master of yon fortress?"

"Castle Trausnitz? Why, Duke Stephen the Grand of the Wittelsbachs! But you can see him yourself in the market square—for today does he judge!"

"My thanks." And I walked Blackspur in her wake, Brandy following at his tail.

So we entered the vast, bustling square. I reined in our mount for Christa and me to study the massive church with its towering steeple stretching toward Heaven; the prosperous, many-storied houses surrounding it; the horse market and rows of stalls—

"*Neiiiiiiiiiiiiigh!*"

Blackspur followed his great trumpet blast with a decisive shake of his head and a rear that scattered all and sundry in fright—and near unseated my sparrow and me.

"Blackspur!" I fought to settle him. "What in God's name—"

"*Hee-haw, hee-haw, hee-haw, hee-haw!*"

"Thomas!" Christa screamed. "John!"

There—across a row of vegetable stalls—our very own Brother Thomas struggled to restrain Martha the donkey, while our very own Brother John dropped all three of his juggling balls, along with his jaw.

The crowd, equally agape, parted like the Red Sea to give access to our joyous reunion with these most excellent friars. Blackspur surged forward, vaulted the coals of a wafer maker—and landed with a snort of satisfaction by Martha's side. Still clutching his reins for dear life, I looked down. Martha's *pregnant* side.

Mercy.

I slid from his back to raise my arms for Christa. She flew from them into the blushing Thomas's embrace, then John's. I waited for my turn. That accomplished, I pointed to Martha. "By Saint Francis himself, how—"

Brother John grinned, softening all the rough angles of his face. "Another Christmas miracle. Before next Christmas, you will be godfather to a mule."

And Blackspur *knew*. Even now the proud father-to-be rubbed his neck against Martha's protruding flanks. I rubbed my own neck. Shrugged my shoulders and laughed. "Well met, good friends!"

"Hell's bells!" Max complained from Brandy's back. "Don't Grock and me rate introductions?"

Grock only delightedly mimicked Martha. *"Hee-haw! Hee-haw!"*

I set him down, and Max followed. Since we all deserved an introduction, I turned to the good friars and the multitude we had assembled. Shook my bells.

"Here to Landshut this day comes a troupe with great cachet!"

I flipped and made a fine sweeping bow.

"Conrad the Good be my name—a jester of indisputable fame!"

Another flip and handstand to Christa.

"My partner be Christof the Fair—of golden voice and golden hair."

A short cartwheel to Max.

"Max of the Second Chance is he—a lad-man with a history. An innocent saved from the gibbet, true villains it is his role to prohibit."

A backflip to Grock.

"Natural fools may come and go, but Grock be steady as a rock. His best test is his sweetness."

Another bow. "Now only see what my company can perform in harmony!"

With a snap of my fingers, Christa, Max, and Grock sprang into their pyramid. Grock waved his horn. Blew.

Ta-da! Ta-da! Ta-da!

The townsfolk laughed and cheered. A few coins were tossed. As I bent to throw them into my empty purse, the crowd stilled, backed off . . . and boots filled my vision. Slowly did I rise to face a brace of liveried guards. A halberd struck sparks on the cobbles before me.

"Stephen the Grand, Elector, bids know who disrupts his great judging duties."

"Disrupt?" I protested. "Our follies do but erupt to toy with natural joy! Forfend the meeting of old friends offend!"

My silver tongue met an impassive face. His weapon shifted ominously. So, too, did his comrade's.

"Come."

"Me?"

"All."

I took "all" to mean my troupe, but the good brothers were also included, as were our mounts. So did we make a pageant through the marketplace to the elector's outdoor court—half the market folk clinging to our rear in curiosity and dismay. Too soon was I before an imposing gentleman— tall, and noble of face and bearing. He sat upon a wooden throne elevated above the crowd, and his stern frown bade no good tidings for me and mine.

Christ's sweet tree! Has it come to this? All our labors, all our trials for naught? Did not one humane lord exist in all of Christendom?

Yet must I try.

I swept into my finest bow, then, unbid, approached the throne.

"Hear me fairly, my lord. My cartwheels grow weak, my rhymes become meek, but yet have I strength to tell you a tale full of sorrow and woe. 'Tis a tale worthy of Arthur, of Siegfried himself—of a quest without ending in search of the best!"

A spark of interest in the great one's eyes—

"What quest you may ask? My answer I give: 'Tis a search with lust for a lord who is just!"

"Proceed."

With that single word, Stephen the Grand burst open the dam of my past. So did I spill forth the holy quest of Conrad the Good, Christof the Fair, Max of the Second Chance, and Grock. So intense was my telling that I hardly noted my loved ones taking their parts in the growing story till their miming tableaux spun and sighed and sang around me. Till Blackspur and lowly Martha and Thomas and John joined themselves with my saga. *Our* saga.

Spent at last, I played my final claim.

"Thus, as you see, a free man I be. I beg you offer liberty—not just to me, but me and mine, for surely without them I'll decline . . . till naught be left but these bells of mine."

A jingle of the bells, a final swoop. I knelt before the throne and bowed my head . . . to hear all of Landshut become a single great sob. As one, they cried—

"Spare him!"

Stephen the Grand held up a hand. "Rise, Conrad the Good." His stern frown softened. "Well spoken. Truly spoken." A pause. "As you have wronged neither me nor my people, there is nothing to spare you from. Free man that you be, I cannot hold you to my lands, but . . ." Now did that severe face crease with smiles. He studied Blackspur still nuzzling his donkey love, then moved his glance to Christa and Max and Grock and the brothers. "I do love rich stories"—he nodded at me—"and nimble tongues."

Then did *the elector,* Duke Stephen the Grand of the Wittelsbachs, spread his arms to encompass us all. "Come, fools and friars. I would you all would feast with me and my court this day. I would you would tarry among us to entertain and preach in Our Lord's holy name—so long as *you* do take joy in the company of *me* and *mine*."

I only stared, my nimble tongue gone mute. It was Christa who saved us. She swept into a bow more graceful than any I'd ever made.

"Gracious Lord Duke, we would be honored to join you and your court."

"Then come forth. I will meet you at Trausnitz anon."

Just so, he excused us to return to his duties. As the crowd closed around, cheering us on, we made our way toward the castle's steep road. Max flipped, again and again. "Christ's love! Does this mean the end of our quest?"

An enlightened ruler? I reached for my sparrow. "God willing, and my words flow free."

Then did Blackspur's mighty neigh of triumph envelop this fool and his family.

AUTHOR'S NOTE

The medieval figure of the fool has fascinated me for years: he of the cockscombed fool's cap with belled donkey ears mischievously flapping; he of the wagging tongue and rude postures. More fascinating still is the concept behind this artificial fool. He imitated the *natural* fool, and in the world of the Middle Ages, these mentally retarded souls were believed to have the ear of God—were believed to be graced with innocent wisdom. Just so, the artificial fool became the lone person within this society who had license *to speak the truth*. What kind of a life could such a jester/fool expect to live? What do my readers really need to know about this existence?

First, the characters in this book are fictional and my own, yet they play their parts within the years of 1365 to 1366. I've re-created these years as truly as I could. It was a hard time to be alive. The life expectancy—if one was fortunate enough to survive infancy and recurrences of the plague—was an average of thirty-four years. People matured early and married early, generally between the ages of fourteen and sixteen. After marriage, the woman's role, be she noble or serf, was to produce as many children as possible. With luck, one or two out of a dozen or more might actually reach adulthood.

It was a violent age, and I haven't downplayed this. The feudal society was absolutely structured in three parts: the Church, which was responsible for the soul; the aristocracy, which was responsible for protection; and the peasantry, which was responsible for feeding everyone. You were born into your place, and there was little chance of escaping it, although by the fourteenth century, the growing merchant classes in the towns were beginning to slowly change this structure. *Freedom* was a frightening word because what it represented might upset the entire applecart. The only members of this tight society who circumvented the system were the wandering minstrels, players—and fools. The thanks they received was to be treated as pariahs. Entertainers *were* forbidden the succor of the Holy Catholic Church. They *were* forbidden the sacraments and were ultimately doomed to be buried in unconsecrated ground. At a time when Heaven, Purgatory, and Hell held more reality than one's few sorry years upon the Middle Earth, this was severe punishment for trying to spread a little joy.

All this said, I'm still fascinated by fools and their possibilities within the medieval system. I hope you'll fall under the spell of Conrad the Good and Christa the Fair and Max of the Second Chance—and my natural fool, Grock, too—as I did while creating them.

A BRIEF BIBLIOGRAPHY

In searching for answers about life in the Middle Ages, I first read Barbara W. Tuchman's superb *A Distant Mirror: The Calamitous 14th Century*. This gave me a broad overview of the period. Next I sought out the fool studies of late nineteenth- and early twentieth-century literary scholars. Classics such as Allardyce Nicoll's *Masks, Mimes and Miracles* gave me a working familiarity with the role itself—as well as with the tricks and japes of the fool's trade. For dialogue patterns, I swallowed whole William Langland's *Piers Plowman* and Geoffrey Chaucer's *The Canterbury Tales*, then modified the speech for contemporary readers. Next did I fall in love again (forgive the fourteenth-century inversion!) with John Ciardi's exquisite translation of Dante's *Inferno*. There were also scholarly tomes on falconry and calendars and dress and . . . too many more topics to mention. I wrapped up my research not in books but by wandering around the castles and museums of Germany—and Landshut itself.